D0193178

I AM CANADA

A CALL TO BATTLE

The War of 1812

by Gillian Chan

Scholastic Canada Ltd.
Toronto New York London Auckland Sydney
Mexico City New Delhi Hong Kong Buenos Aires

While the events described and some of the characters in this book may be based on actual historical events and real people, Alexander MacKay is a fictional character created by the author, and his journal is a work of fiction.

A Dear Canada Book. Published by Scholastic Canada Ltd.

Library and Archives Canada Cataloguing in Publication

Chan, Gillian
A call to battle : The War of 1812 / by Gillian Chan.

(I am Canada)
ISBN 978-1-4431-0006-9

1. Canada--History--War of 1812--Juvenile fiction.
I. Title. II. Series: I am Canada

PS8555.H39243C35 2012 jC813'.54 C2012-901667-5

6 5 4 3 2 1 Printed in Canada 114 12 13 14 15 16

The display type was set in Albertus.
The text was set in Minion.

First printing September 2012

In memory of Jimmy Durrant 1921–2010
A wonderful father

Prologue

August 1820

I've known for six long years that I would have to make this journey. I've known it because I promised Father I would when we stood in the trees on the edge of Lundy's Lane, as the sun burned off the mist, revealing the dead and the dying where they still lay.

It's not a journey I've wanted to make until now, but Fortune has smiled upon me and I have another reason to go, one that will secure my future and my place in the world. It too can be traced to that bloody battlefield.

For days now Mother has been fluttering around like a hen with wet feathers, constantly telling me that I must remember to be careful on the road, to not take up with any ruffians, and to keep my money hidden in the secret pocket she sewed into my jacket, along with the letter from the Phillips family. Anyone would think I was just a boy like my brother Samuel, instead of a twenty-one-year-old. She forgets that I fought alongside Father and Angus in the War when I was just fifteen. Ah, that's unfair — we never did tell her all. She would not have been able to bear it. She knows it was bad, though. She saw what happened to Angus; saw how Father has been aged by it all. Even now I do not like to think too hard on it, but now I must, because what happened to me then lies at the root of this journey I must make to Pennsylvania.

I was thirteen when war broke out, big for my age — the same size as my brother Angus, though he was five years older. I was broader and stronger, too, like my grandfather. I can see that our nearness in height was just about the only similarity between us. Angus was sunny-natured — nothing angered him, and he was not given to anything sudden. Me, I was loud and complaining, quick to act, with little thought as to what might come of my actions. When I look back, I am amazed at what I dared and the punishments I courted. I resented the way that no one paid me the slightest attention except to give me orders or to reprimand me when I did wrong. I was just the family work-horse, expected to help out on our farm all day with Angus and Father, yet treated as a child on all other occasions.

I remember clearly the day we got news that the Yankees had declared war on us, and how angry I was by the end of it. I grew up on tales of war — Father had fought for the British in Butler's Rangers during the Revolutionary War. Mother's brother Roger, too. I liked nothing better than when Angus and I could persuade Father to tell us tales of how he had fought so fiercely for seven years until he mustered out. The stories of how he came here to the Head of the Lake to carve out a home for us were less exciting, but he would not tell one without the other.

I knew that I was ready for such thrilling adventures myself, that I would acquit myself nobly and bravely, if given the chance.

Those memories rise unbidden and freely now and I must honour them, too.

Chapter 1
June 1812

Father, Angus and I were working on framing another room on the side of the house. Mother and my two older sisters, Morag and Polly, had got hold of a fancy notion that they wanted a parlour. A horse came barrelling down from the road to the clearing where our house stood. We heard its hooves, but with it being so dry and hot, such a great cloud of dust was raised that it was hard to see who was coming, until he pulled on the reins to stop his horse and dismounted.

It was Callum Murdoch, the teacher who had set up a school in our village. He and Father had been talking about my going there after the harvest was in, but surely this was not the reason for such a wild ride.

"Robert! Angus!" he called. "Have you heard?" His face was flushed and his eyes shone with excitement.

Conflicting emotions warred within me. I was intrigued that he obviously had news important enough to bring him racing out to our farm, but furious that once again I was being ignored.

Mother, Morag and Polly had come out from the house at the noise. Any visitor was an event. Polly blushed when she saw who it was. She had been sweet on Mr. Murdoch since she'd danced with him at a harvest supper at my Uncle William's farm.

Mr. Murdoch was grinning. "By your blank faces, I'll wager you've not. Sam Hatt said I'd better come, as you'd not been by his mill for days." His grin widened. "The militia are to muster. The American president has declared war on us!"

He continued talking, but I let loose with a volley of "Huzzahs!" and shook my fist in the air. That lazy, little ruffian Drew appeared from behind the barn, where he had probably been skulking. He, too, whooped and hollered. Even Samuel pounded his wooden rattle on the boards of the porch.

"Be quiet, you stupid boy!" my father bellowed. He dropped the hammer he was holding, and his arms hung limp at his sides. He exchanged a look with Mother. Her face had paled and I swear that her chin trembled. Father glared at me, and I was hard pressed not to cry. I did not understand. Shouldn't he be pleased that we would have a chance to pay back the Yankees for the harm they had done our family, and proud that I showed such spirit?

"Father," I said, trying to make my words ring out, "I may not have the years, but my size and strength equal any grown man's. I will fight, too!"

Mother let out a small moan and Father rushed over to her. "You're still a child, Sandy, as your thoughtlessness proves." His face had flushed with anger and his voice shook. "Go and stay with the little ones while Angus and I talk with Mr. Murdoch. Morag and Polly, see to your mother."

How dare he treat me so? I stalked up to the porch and grabbed Samuel, who immediately wailed, but I didn't care. "Ellen, Drew, come with me," I ordered as I moved in the direction of the barn, trying to stay within hearing distance of Angus, Father and Mr. Murdoch. It was hard to hear what they said because Ellen and Drew, being the pestilential brats that they were, kept up a clamour of questions about what was to happen. Father's face darkened when Mr. Murdoch said that some of the men he had called on were reluctant to fight, worried about their crops or perhaps even secretly in sympathy with our enemy. Father had no time for such men and was a proud sergeant in the flank company of the 5th Lincoln, chosen for his patriotism and sense of duty. Angus was his younger, mirror image.

After Mr. Murdoch left, Father remained sombre for the rest of the day, abandoning our work on the house and taking Angus away into the woods, muskets in hand. I looked hopefully at Father, silently praying that he might ask me to go with them, if only to hone my shooting skills. Ever since I was big enough to hold a musket, he had taught me, and I swear that I was his equal when it came to marksmanship, better than Angus even. But he did not even glance in my direction and I was too proud to ask, especially after his earlier rebuke. Instead I just bit my lip, thinking that I might manage to slip away and at least watch them.

Mother spent the day sobbing in the kitchen with Morag and Polly trying hard to calm her. The girls had retrieved the baby from me and I hoped I might put my plan into action. Luck was not with me. Morag emerged just as I was drifting towards the woods and ordered me to spend the rest of the day tending our vegetable plots, work she and Polly usually did and which I despised. I looked round for Drew and Ellen, intending to press them into helping me, but, canny as ever, they were nowhere in sight — Drew had likely led Ellen away somewhere to avoid work. I was so angry, it was not only weeds that got pulled. I had to come up with a way to persuade Father to let me go with him and Angus when they marched for the Niagara River with their company. By the time we were all seated for supper, I thought I had a convincing argument to make.

Mother was no longer crying, but her eyes were red and she clutched Samuel tightly on her lap, kissing his curls every so often, as Morag and Polly served our meal. Normally our meals are lively, but for this one we took our cue from Father, who sat silent as he methodically chewed his food, his eyes apparently seeing nothing but his plate. I could hardly eat, waiting for him to say something so I could plead my case and change his mind.

With the last bite eaten, Father finally laid down his fork and patted Mother's hand. When he spoke, his voice was steady and he looked round the table at each of us. "My children, you heard the news that Callum Murdoch brought today and you know that we are living in unsettled times. I must ask you all to come together so that we can face them and come through stronger than before. Angus and I will leave tomorrow to join our regiment, so it will fall to you older ones,

Morag and Polly, to help your mother keep the farm running, and to look after the wee ones." Father paused and looked directly at me. "Sandy, you will be the backbone of the farm, taking on the work your brother and I do."

I tried to protest, but he cut me off. "It will be hard, but your sisters will work in the fields when they can and you will be able to turn to your Uncle William for help and advice, should you need it. He's too old and lame to fight." Father paused, then looked at Drew, his voice soft but stern. "Andrew, you can no longer play as much now. You're a big strong boy for your age and it's time for you to do your share and listen to your elders more. Sandy will help teach you the outside work that needs to be done."

I was pleased that Father realised Drew was a lazy rascal, and using his full name showed how serious he was, but I could not let him continue. I had to speak. "Father, you *have* to let me go with you. I can fight as well as any. You know what a good marksman I am, thanks to your training. You've said how large and strong I am. I know I should be sixteen to join the militia, but they would take me with your permission, I know they would. Younger boys have gone, some even instead of their fathers. Mother and the girls can manage for the time it will take us to send those cowardly Yankees packing. Mr. Murdoch even said that some men hereabouts are laggards who do not want to fight. Let me take their place. I beg you, Father, please say I can fight!"

Father didn't shout this time, just shook his head wearily. "Sandy, war is not a glorious game. It's no place for a boy with a head full of dreams. Our crops need to be tended and it's because of your size and strength that I need you here. You may be young but you can do the work of a grown man, and it will be one less worry for me while I am away." He sighed. "Not everyone can say that, and I can understand why there will be those who will not answer their call to duty."

When I tried to argue, Father held up his hand. "Enough, Sandy! I will not debate this with you."

I could not help the tears that sprang into my eyes, and hung my head so they could not be seen. I heard what Father said, knew that he meant it, but his words did not dampen my anger. I *would* go, somehow.

The next day, Father and Angus made their goodbyes as the sun was just rising. They were dressed alike in linen shirts, already damp with sweat, with their muskets slung over their shoulders and a bag of shot. Each had a rolled, wool blanket and Angus was carrying a small sack of provisions that Mother had put together, while Father had their water skin.

After her tears of the day before, I was surprised to see Mother dry-eyed. Her voice was steady and gave no sign of her worries, although her words did. She leaned into Father, one arm around his waist, her other hand reaching up to gently touch Angus's cheek. "Rob, you take care. And I need you to bring my boy back to me."

"That I will, Hannah. I promise." Father looked over at the rest of us where we stood on the porch, as if he wanted to memorise each and every one. "Come say goodbye," he said, and held out his arms.

The others all hurried over to be hugged, but I hung back. Father did not say anything, just let his arms drop to his side as he looked steadily at me.

Mother's face coloured red and she moved towards me, grabbing my arm and pulling at me. "Enough of this sulking, Sandy. It ill becomes you. Now make your farewells to your father and brother!"

I allowed myself to smile. "If I am big enough to work like a man, I'm too big to be hugged like a child." The words tasted bad in my mouth, but I could not help myself.

Mother reached up to try and cuff my ear, but her blow was weak and fell short, merely grazing my shoulder. Her tears had returned and choked her voice. "You're a stubborn, nasty boy and I hope that you will not come to regret your actions today, Alexander!"

I said nothing, just turned and walked to where I had left my hoe, picked it up and headed towards our fields. I did not look back.

Chapter 2
Fall 1812

It was several months before we saw Father and Angus.

Those months seemed a never-ending haze of work for Drew and myself, although Morag worked in the fields alongside us, leaving Mother and Polly to tend to the house and garden. We were up at sunrise and never seemed to stop until sundown, gulping down our food and going to bed, only for the whole round to start again the next morning. Drew surprised me. He whined at first and cried a little when he could not go roaming in the woods with Ellen, but soon he was no longer a hindrance but a help, a pair of hands always there and willing. Morag, too, proved herself as good as many men. She borrowed a pair of Angus's breeches and an old shirt he had left behind. Before we started work she would hide in the woods at the edge of the field to change into them, for if Mother had seen her dressed like a boy she would have had a conniption. I was proud that we got our harvest in, and a bumper one at that, with just a little help from Uncle William, who came for only one day with his hired man.

Where we missed Angus and Father most was the accounts. I was a better scholar than most. Father had made sure of that, making us all practise our letters and numbers, and whereas I might chafe at spending evenings doing this, such things came easily to me, more than they did to Angus, who had to work far harder. He was diligent and less hasty than I was and his neat script and orderly columns of figures made my blot-and-cross-filled efforts look very poor indeed.

What I liked most were the books that Father at first read to us, and which I later was able to read myself: histories and verse. Before the war broke out, Father had said that he could teach me no more and if we had the money I could perhaps go to the school that Callum Murdoch ran in Ancaster.

When some of the militia came back only days after they had left, I could see how it pained Mother that Father and Angus were not among them. Her worry grew when news slowly filtered back of fighting at Detroit, and then at Queenston. The Macdonnells in Cootes Paradise were grey-faced at our Sunday services after learning that their son Martyn had died from wounds he received. Martyn was the same age as Angus, and I know that even as Mother comforted Mrs. Macdonnell, she was fighting to keep her fears for her own son in check.

As her worry grew I will admit that mine did, too, when others who had been wounded made their way back. Callum Murdoch was just such a one and we all prayed for him as his life hung in the balance for what seemed like a month. Only the devoted nursing of Amy Mason and Callum's family pulled him through, although he would never walk without a limp and would certainly never fight with the Lincolns again.

At dinner, we often talked of what news had come, and wondered why we had had none from Father. One night, Mother shook her head ruefully when Ellen asked when Father and Angus were coming home. "Your father has always had a strong sense of duty, Ellen. If they call for volunteers to stay, he will be the first, with Angus but a beat behind him."

"I'd be like that, too, if only I had been allowed to go!" I said.

Mother sighed. "I know, Sandy. No one doubts you, but you are needed here, and a fine job you've been doing, too." She forced a smile, but then grew serious again. "It's the not knowing that is so hard to bear. No matter what I am doing, my mind is always with them, wondering where they are and whether they are safe."

I knew what Mother meant, as I hungered for news as well, but it was the progress of the war and whether there might be an opportunity for me to become part of it that were foremost in my mind, not how my father and brother fared.

My visits to the Red Mill were the only bright spots in my existence. Sam Hatt and his brother, Richard, the owners of the mill, served in the 5th Lincoln, too — although they were officers, as befit their standing in our community — so the mill was the best source for news. It was there that I heard of Tecumseh and General Brock's cunning ruse in tricking the Americans at Fort Detroit, by having Tecumseh's men appear to be a much larger force. I laughed as Mr. Hatt described how Brock had had them run in and out of the woods, shrieking and yelling. There was much ill feeling between the Yankees and Tecumseh's men, whom they feared for their viciousness both in fighting and its aftermath. The Americans were so afraid of what the warriors might do if they were victorious, Governor Hull surrendered the fort, and a large store of weapons, to a force much smaller than his own.

Mr. Hatt himself, home for a while to manage his affairs, told me what a stalwart my father was, how the younger men looked up to him. It reassured me that he and Angus were all right — news that would calm Mother and the girls — and which made me glow with pride.

It was at the mill, too, that news of the glorious but sad victory at Queenston, and of the loss of brave General Brock, came. I had so many questions and they came bursting from me, but apart from telling me that Father had come through unscathed while Angus had had a musket ball part his hair for him, Mr. Hatt was not forthcoming, turning his attention to other customers as if I were of little account. I seethed with anger, wanting to know more, wanting to tell him that my father had ordered me to tend the farm — otherwise I would have been there, too, and likely in the thick of the fighting. I went home in a fine temper at the injustice of my situation and poor Drew bore the worst of it as I ordered him around and found fault with everything he did, in my frustration.

When I passed this news on to Mother and the girls, they cried to hear of Angus's close call. Mother cried even more when I told her that Father and Angus would not be home until the start of December, being on garrison duty at Fort George until then, guarding prisoners. I could not work out whether these were tears of sadness or happiness. For my part I would be glad to have Father home. I could try again to persuade him to let me go back with them, now that the harvest was in and Drew was working so hard. Surely he and Morag could manage the outside work without me.

When Callum Murdoch was finally recovered enough to attend a Sunday service at the Shavers' farm, I heard nothing of the sermon from the visiting preacher because I was burning to find out all that had happened at Queenston. As soon as the after-sermon visiting started, I made my way immediately to where Callum sat on a bale of straw, Amy by his side. I was shocked by how thin he had become, and winced when he dragged himself up to a standing position using a crutch that Amy passed to him.

"You want news of your father and brother, I'll wager," Callum said before I even had a chance to open my mouth. "I'm sure that you've already heard that they both came through unharmed, although Angus did have a close call!" He grimaced in pain as he shifted his weight, leaning more heavily on the crutch.

"We did," I said, "but . . . " and I hesitated, not wishing to appear crass in my eagerness. "What was it like? To fight, I mean?"

Callum's smile faded. "Nothing like you might imagine it to be, young Sandy. I was not with your father and brother, as I was with a group under Sam Hatt who were guarding guns at Vrooman's Point, just north of the village. When the gun on the Redan Battery fell to the Americans, we were all that was left, firing at the American boats as they tried to cross the river." He smiled ruefully. "Not that we were doing much good, as the distance was too great for accuracy."

"But you were holding fast?" I said, eager for more details.

"Oh aye, we did. When the troops retreated, carrying poor General Brock, it was near our position they formed up."

"You *saw* Brock?" I wanted so much to hear of the hero of Detroit. "Did you hear him speak any brave last words?"

"I saw him, Sandy, carried by his men, but he was long dead by the time they arrived."

I was disappointed, wanting to hear of General Brock exhorting his men on to glory and to revenge his death.

Callum patted my shoulder. My disappointment must have shown in my face, for he said, "He was very brave, Sandy. He had no thought of his own safety, or so his men said — he charged the enemy with his sword in hand until he was shot down. And if you want heroes, then look no further than Captain Norton and his Mohawks! They scaled the heights by way of an overgrown track, and surprised the Americans. Even though they were driven back at first, they persisted, and such is the fear they engender, the Americans lost heart." He stopped as a fit of coughing overtook him. I waited patiently, hoping for more. This was just the type of derring-do I knew I would have if only Father let me join him and Angus.

Amy glared at me. "Enough, Callum," she said. "This is the first time out since your sick bed. You must not overtire yourself." When Callum seemed likely to stumble, she turned on me and said, "Make yourself useful, Sandy. Instead of questions, help me get Callum to our wagon."

She might have been little in stature but she was fierce, and I did as I was told, supporting Callum as best I could. He leaned heavily on me, and as I boosted him up onto the wagon's seat, he managed a smile and said, "We will talk more, Sandy, I promise."

I hoped that we would, as I had so many questions still. What had Father and Angus been doing, how had Callum been wounded, and how proud was he of all that he had done?

Once December came, we all were on tenterhooks, waiting for Father and Angus, or at least for some news that they were on their way home. None came. The atmosphere in our home was sour and sad. I preferred to spend my time in the barn with Drew, threshing oats. Then one morning I heard a commotion in front of the house — Mother screaming as if someone had wounded her. Drew and I raced out of the barn to find her supported by the girls, all of them crying. A stranger was standing there, holding his horse by the reins, looking more than a little aghast at the weeping women in front of him.

I drew myself to my full height and tried to speak in my deepest tones, praying that my voice would not crack and squeak, as it was prone to do. The man was unarmed, but a musket was tied to his saddle. "Sir, might I ask your business? Business that seems to have upset my family."

"You have my apologies." The man spoke with the same Scottish burr as Father. "I have the unhappy task of being the bearer of bad news."

A wave of dread washed over me.

"I was travelling up to York and stopped the night at Forty Mile Creek at a farm owned by the Van Camp family. They asked me to amend my journey to seek out the family of a Robert and Angus MacKay and bring news of them." He paused. "They were on their way home to you when the older one was taken ill."

Mother let out another wail.

"Van Camp has given them shelter in his barn, but he wants them off the property quickly lest they share the contagion they have brought with them." He spat then and grimaced. "Van Camp is a hard man, with little kindness about him, and I fear that he will turn them out if someone does not go for them soon."

I had never felt such a mix of emotion — relief that Father and Angus were alive, but also worry about the situation they now found themselves in. Thoughts were racing through my head. If I set out now with the horses and wagon, I could be at Forty Mile Creek before night fell . . . What illness could make my Father unable to travel? . . . Would we need to seek out Dr. Tiffany — often a hard job, as he ranged the countryside treating the sick.

I did not hesitate. "I'll go. Drew, go harness the horses and ready the wagon."

I turned to the stranger. "I thank you, sir, for bringing us this news." For a moment, I was at a loss as to what else to say, but then I thought of what Father would do. "If you have the time to spare, my family would be happy to provide you with a meal before you resume your journey."

He smiled then. "A kind offer, but I have business with George Rousseau at his hotel in the village and must make my way there now." With that he remounted and, with a click of his tongue to the horse, was on his way, leaving our family shattered in his passing.

"Sandy." Morag stepped off the porch. "Let me come with you, or at least let me send for Uncle William. It is a long journey to make on your own."

"No, I'll do this," I said. "You will do better here. I don't want to waste time waiting for our uncle to arrive. Send Drew to see if Dr. Tiffany is at home and ask him to come here tomorrow, late in the afternoon, if he can. If all goes well, I will set off for home at first light tomorrow to bring Father and Angus back here."

Drew was quick in readying the wagon, but I was not allowed the speedy getaway I wanted. Polly and Morag hastily gathered together blankets and a straw tick, while Mother put bread, cheese, some cold chicken, and scones into a basket, along with stone jugs of whisky and water.

It was a bright but cold mid-morning by the time I set out. I was grateful, as it meant that the trail would not be a slough of mud to slow me down, and I had time to sink into my own thoughts. What could be wrong with Father? It sounded bad. He had always been strong, rarely ill, but he was no longer a young man. I saw no one on the trail until close to Forty Mile Creek, when I passed a farmer who was able to direct me to the Van Camp farm just as dusk was falling.

As my wagon rattled over the rutted track, I marvelled at the farm ahead. Broad fields lay winter fallow around a spacious house made of stone. I had thought our wooden house fine, but this was like something you might see in a city. Several outbuildings, also stone, lay to one side.

Even before I had time to get down from the wagon, a short, bearded man with a lantern in his hand came out from the house. "Are you a MacKay?" he demanded. Without waiting for an answer, he continued, "You have the look of them — big lummoxes both."

A girl about my age had come out, too. She stood framed in the doorway, clutching a shawl tightly around her shoulders. She looked scared, and I saw her shiver as her father raised his voice to speak again.

"I'd not have allowed your kin to stay had I known what contagion they brought with them, but it was already night and there was a threat of snow."

He noticed the girl then. "Mathilda, get back inside at once." When she hesitated, he took a step towards her, his fist raised, staying like that until she slunk back into the house.

"Can you take me to them?" I stepped towards the house, but Van Camp waved me back.

"Come no closer. They are in the barn." He spat on the ground ahead of my feet. "All soldiers are filthy and licentious. The militia, too," he said. "Even healthy, I would not have them around my womenfolk."

"Sir," I said, struggling to keep my anger from flaring, "my father is a well-respected man in our village, who gladly serves the king to protect our country from the Americans. He and my brother fought bravely at Queenston."

"A patriot," Van Camp snorted. "There are some of us who think it would be better if we threw off the yoke of the British."

"That's treasonous talk!" The words flew out of my mouth, and before I had the chance to say more, Van Camp stepped forward and cracked me across the mouth with his open hand, rocking me where I stood.

"Shut your mouth, whelp!" He pointed to the

furthest outbuilding. "They're in there. I'll be reasonable and not turn you out in the night, but understand this. I want you gone by first light. You can feed and water your horses, but don't expect anything else and do not come to the house for any reason."

When I went to speak, he pointed his finger at me. "No more," he said. "I will not hear your puling words."

I headed into the barn, dreading what might await me there.

At first it was hard to see, for the building had only one small, shuttered window. In the far corner a candle flickered, enough that I could make out the shapes of my father and brother. Angus sat with his back against the wall, his head in his hands, but looked up as I stepped inside. Father was on the floor alongside Angus, his head resting on a blanket roll. The blanket covering him was pulled awry as he twisted and turned, his body racked with tremors.

"Sandy, oh, Sandy!" Angus sprang to his feet and clutched me to him. He smelled rank, sweat mingling with wood smoke. "I've been praying all day that someone would come, but I thought it would be Uncle William."

"Father! What's wrong with Father?" I pulled myself free and knelt down beside him.

Angus stood behind me, one hand resting on my shoulder. He must have felt the shudder that shook me as I regarded Father, for he gripped my shoulder even more tightly. Father's face was flushed, stippled with red dots. He was sweat-soaked, his hair lying in wet strands across his face. His eyes were open but he did not seem to see us. His mouth moved, but I didn't understand the words that came out of it.

"I think it's Gaelic," Angus said, kneeling down beside me but not letting loose his grip on my shoulder. "The language he spoke in Scotland. He's been like this for two days now. I've tried bathing his face with cold water and I've got some water into him, too, but that's all I've been able to do. He won't eat and I don't know what we can do other than get him home and out of this hellhole." Angus's face was sombre. "Van Camp wants no truck with us, scared that whatever Father has will be passed on. It's gaol fever, I think, caught from the prisoners and — " Angus's voice faltered here " — I've seen more of them die than recover."

I had no words to comfort Angus. "I'll bring you some food that Mother sent. Perhaps Father will eat some, too. I'll tend to the horses, then come in and watch over Father while you get some sleep, which I warrant you've not had these last two days. You need to be rested when we leave first thing."

He smiled — just a ghost of his usual broad grin — but said nothing and took up his position by Father again.

I was so frightened that it consumed me as I went through the routine of unharnessing and then taking the horses to drink from the trough of icy water in front of the barn. I almost didn't hear the low whistle. Startled, I looked round. There, pressed up against the wall of the barn, was the girl I had seen earlier. Mathilda. I started towards her, but she motioned me to stay where I was.

"Keep working on your horses," she said in a low whisper. "My father would beat me if he saw me talking to you. I've got a bowl of broth here. When I'm gone, take it and give it to your brother for your father. My father says there may be snow tonight, and you'll need something to warm you up. Hide the bowl in the straw when you're done, and I will take it up later."

Before I could thank her, she drifted away in the direction of the house. I got the horses settled in the barn, their whickering telling me that they were content, even if a little spooked by their strange surroundings and the presence of Van Camp's horses. I retrieved the bowl from the foot of the wall and draped my open jacket around it so it could not be seen.

Angus smiled when I told him of our unexpected gift. "She's kind." he said. "It was only through her pleading that her father allowed us to spend the night here in the first place, and that was before Father took sick." His face grew sad. "I think she paid for it. Her face was bruised the next time I saw her. We've been lucky, Sandy, not to have a father quick with his fists."

I didn't dare tell Angus that Van Camp had struck me. We would be safely on our way before he saw the bruises that surely would develop.

Angus reached inside his pack for a spoon and tried to feed Father the broth, but to no avail. Father clamped his lips shut and turned his head away. Soup trickled down in his whiskers and Angus wiped it away with a grimy handkerchief.

"If he won't take it, you have it, Angus," I said, conscious of how thin he had become. "Then try to sleep."

It was a long, hard night. Angus did sleep some, perhaps an hour or two, but I could not as I watched Father, whose restless movement and muttering did not slow down. Once Angus realised I was not sleeping, he shifted so that he sat next to me, our backs against the wall. I wanted to ask whether he thought Father would pull through, but I could not bring myself to say it, in case the answer he gave was the one I dreaded. Instead, I asked him about the fighting he'd seen, burning to hear of the glory of it all, how our brave troops had routed the Americans so easily.

Angus didn't answer at first. He stared straight ahead and frowned before he finally spoke. "It's hard, Sandy, to find words to describe it." He stopped, as if he were looking for those words. "We were in Queenston village and we'd been given so much guard duty at night, we were hardly awake when the Americans attacked in the early hours. I just kept my head down and did what Father told me, fired my musket when he told me to, ran when he said we should run. Others followed him, too, in all that confusion." He laughed then. "It was well I did — keep my head down, that is — for once, as we ran, musket balls flying all around us like shooting stars, one grazed the top of my hair." He pointed to the top of his head. "You can see the scorch mark there still."

Angus paused. "You cannot imagine what it was like, Sandy. It's confused in my mind even now with the noise, the movement and shouting. The British had retreated from the heights to the village and we were all firing from the shelter of houses. American guns had the measure of the village and were bombarding it. By mid-morning I thought we were done for. The Yankees had managed to turn our own gun on the Redan against us. Some stormed into the village, looting the houses and managing to free the prisoners we had taken. We bided our time, skulking, shooting when we could, until British reinforcements arrived from Fort George."

I wanted even more than this drab tale that Angus was telling me. "But Angus, did you do any great deed?" I asked. "Did you save someone's life, or kill any Yankees single-handed? Were you there when General Brock died leading a charge on the heights?"

Angus shook his head. "No." He smiled. "Not that that would stop half the Lincolns who were with me from telling you that not only did they *see* him die, but they cradled him in their arms and heard his last words." The smile faded from his face and his voice became quieter. "I survived, Sandy, and that was enough. We were left to guard the village when the British and some militia counterattacked in the afternoon, so I cannot tell you what happened. Maybe Callum Murdoch might, for he was there . . . if he's recovered." Angus's voice rose in question and he shuddered, perhaps fearing the answer he might get.

"He is," I said fervently, wanting to see my brother's usual sunny smile, which seemed to have vanished in the time he'd been away. "I saw him at the Sunday meeting, just a week ago. He will always limp and he looks much weakened."

Angus ran his hand over his face. "Then he lives. Oh, that is good news. I feared for him, Sandy. In the end, it's said that we sent them packing, but truthfully, I'm not sure we did. It would be better to say that we outlasted them. They had not the heart nor support to press on."

Father groaned and we both looked down, thinking perhaps he was awake, but we were disappointed.

Angus patted my arm. "We should try to sleep. It will be a difficult journey home tomorrow." He lay down on the straw beside Father.

I sat up a while longer, thinking about what Angus said, knowing that I would not follow Father so blindly when it came my turn to fight. I would be the one to bring glory to the MacKay name.

By the time the sun struggled to pierce the early morning clouds, we were both exhausted, but at least Father seemed no worse. We loaded him gently into the back of the wagon. He had soiled himself, and this combined with the foul smell of his sweat made it hard to be by him. Angus drove the wagon while I sat in the back, trying to keep Father calm and comfortable. It was not an easy task. Whether the movement of the wagon hurt him or agitated him, I do not know, but he became more and more restless, flailing his arms, kicking and, one time, struggling to his feet, only to fall heavily back down. I have never been so glad to see the track that led to our home.

Drew was the first to hear us coming. He raced out from the house yelling, "They're here, they're here! Sandy has fetched them home safe!" He ran alongside us, still shouting, until we drew to a halt in front of the house and Mother and the girls came running out, followed by the tall, angular form of Dr. Tiffany. Mother stifled a sob when she peered into the wagon and saw the state Father was in, but the girls had no such control. Ellen alone was dry-eyed. I'm sure she had no idea how her words stung when she looked at Mother and asked, "Is Father dying? Have they brought him home to die?"

Mother's voice was soft, but there was steely determination in it, too. "No, Ellen, we will not let him die. Is that not right, Doctor?"

Dr. Tiffany hesitated before replying. "We will all do our best," he said. "Now, let's get poor Rob inside."

Father was thrashing around again, so it took all the strength we had to manhandle him inside so that Mother and the doctor could treat him. When I went outside to see to the wagon and horses, Angus made as if to go with me, but I sent him in, too — he was tired, dirty and starved. I sent Drew for buckets of water from the well to sluice down the wagon bed and wash away the filth. We worked in silence and although I knew we finally had it clean, it was as if the stench still lingered in my nostrils, a stench that frightened me to the core of my being.

* * *

Those next months were consumed by Father's illness, which lingered and lingered, sucking the life from him until he seemed a hollow version of the man he had been. Typhus was what Dr. Tiffany called it, and agreed with Angus that it was likely caught from those damn Yankee prisoners they had been guarding — although, being a Yankee himself, Dr. Tiffany did not call them that! For days, and then weeks, Father burned with fever, often not knowing where he was, not recognising Mother, who never seemed to leave his side. She even slept on a straw tick alongside their bed. Nothing Dr. Tiffany tried — bleeding him with leeches, or making him vomit — helped. Finally, Mother called a halt to it all, saying that the treatments made Father a little weaker each time and that rest and wholesome food would have to do the trick.

Angus, too, came down with it, but perhaps his youth saved him from the worst, because after a week of fever — a week when I thought that without Morag and Polly, Mother would have driven herself into exhaustion — he recovered quickly and soon was back working with me.

He would not talk more of what had befallen him and Father, no matter how much I begged him.

Chapter 3
May 1813

It was not until the spring came that Father regained some semblance of health. By early April he was sitting on the porch — a little gaunt, to be sure, and his hair had become as grey as his brother William's — but he was himself. Each day that passed saw more colour come back to his face. By May he worked alongside us, although Angus and I were quick to help him, if we could do it without him realising what we were doing.

Angus was now the one to do all the errands off the farm. I hated how little news he brought back from these trips or how, when he did have some, he would make sure that he took Father aside to tell him. It annoyed me so much that I challenged him about this, but all he did was smile and say that he wanted to make sure that if it were bad news, such as when the American forces captured York in April, he would not scare Mother and the girls. He did not want the rumours swirling about — men were saying that the Americans would try to push up from Niagara — to colour our lives with fear.

I could see that the news was bad, but it just fuelled the fire of my wanting to fight, too. I listened where I could and pieced together what had happened at York. The Americans had landed from the lake and it shamed me to hear that the decision to retreat was made so quickly by the British commander. At least before he left he blew up the Grand Magazine containing, so they say, five hundred barrels of gunpowder! The American commander and many soldiers were killed by the mighty blast and people said this was why the Americans had looted and burned in York — terrorising its inhabitants in revenge. They eventually withdrew, for they could not hope to hold the town with no support coming. But American forces still pressed hard in Niagara, taking Fort George. And what had the British there done? They retreated to Burlington Heights!

It seemed foolish and cowardly. No one, militia or regular, should rest until every last Yankee had been driven back across the border! I was determined to be ready and, whenever I had the chance, if I saw that Father was occupied, I'd sneak his musket out and go through the movements of loading it, trying to make myself as speedy as I could.

The end of May gave me an opportunity to show Father how grown I was, the equal of most men, when we were invited to Uncle William's farm. Though it was large and well established, he wanted to push back the forest some more to enlarge his fields, so he sent word out inviting all in the district to a clearing bee.

The whole family was excited, as we would go and have a chance to visit with our friends and neighbours. Uncle William's wife had died two years ago and he had only sons yet unmarried, so he asked Mother and the girls to supervise the food. This they gladly did, baking so much that I feared there would be little room in the wagon for Drew and Ellen and Sam!

After days of rain and cold, the day of the bee was bright and clear — warm, but not so hot as to be oppressive. We had gone the night before, and it seemed as if morning had barely arrived before wagons full of people started to arrive. Mother and the girls were kept busy, as each new arrival came forward with food, which they laid out on trestle tables in the shade. Drew and Ellen had been put to work turning the spit for the roasting piglets. Uncle William appointed Father the grog boss — a wise choice, as he would have the sense to make sure that no man went thirsty, but he would not let any man drink too much until the clearing had been done. It was kind of Uncle William, too, as it gave Father a way to participate without feeling left out of the action. He had always been in the thick of anything like this.

When the teams were made up for the clearing, I hung back, not sure whether I would be included. I didn't want to be humiliated if I should step forward, only to be told that there was no place for me because of my age. Angus, who had been named as head of one team, caught my eye and beckoned me over, but I was still reluctant. My hesitation must have been apparent because my uncle shouted out, "Not so fast, Angus!"

He turned and winked at the men around him. "Two MacKays on the same team is hardly fair, is it? Not with the size of them!" He grasped my shoulder and pulled me to him. "Now, who wants this fine specimen to work for them?" He twirled me round as if I were a bull he was trying to sell. I coloured red, but was secretly pleased. My smile grew even broader when each of the three other teams began calling out that they wanted me. Finally, after much bantering back and forth, it was decided that I would join Benjamin Smith's Green Team. They pulled me into their midst and clapped me on the back as they told me what a fine fellow I was and what a great help to my father I'd been both while he was away and during his illness.

I couldn't help but laugh a little as Drew dropped the spit handle and rushed forward, demanding not to be left with the girls and little children, as he was quite big and strong enough to work with me, too . . . and how crestfallen he looked when he was sent packing.

The day before, Uncle William and his sons had marked the area to be cleared, dividing it into four equal segments, each marked at its corners by rags of blue, green, yellow and red. It was more brush than true forest, so there were few tall trees to be chopped down, but those we tackled first. I was flattered when Ben Smith handed me his axe, saying, "Sandy, you're the biggest and youngest amongst us, so let's give you the most onerous task." I just wished that Father had been there to see how I was treated like a grown man rather than a boy!

It took me only a little time to bring down that first tree and I had not even raised a sweat when it was time to move on to the second. Behind me the other men on my team were cutting the tree down to size, lopping off its branches and sawing its trunk into manageable pieces. Others were chopping the bushes and then pulling up their roots, leaving a swath of cleared land behind us. From the shouts, I could hear that the other teams were making good progress, too. Angus's Blue Team was the one closest to us; he was their main axe man as well. With the last of the tall trees down, I set about making myself as useful as I could. It soon became clear that I was best suited to loading the sled with the cut wood, then pulling it back to the woodpile that was rapidly growing beside Uncle William's barn. On my second return, Father and Drew were there with a cask of whisky and a cask of water, doling out a cupful to each man as he worked. I expected to be handed the water only, but was surprised when Father offered me a cup of whisky, too. It burned as it went down and I was hard pressed not to splutter and choke, but my pride would not let me do so.

"It's a two-team race," Father said as I handed the tin cup back to him. "Blue and Green are far ahead of Yellow and Red, and you and Angus are a credit to your teams. It makes me proud to have two such strong sons. I swear that you have grown even more, Sandy."

Ben Smith, who was standing close, called out, "He has inches on Angus. He is even taller than you, MacKay."

Father shook his head, "No, I've still got the measure of him."

"You're wrong. He's taller and he is certainly broader. Let's settle this. The two of you stand back to back." Smith was grinning as he motioned us to get into the position he desired.

Father felt slight against my back, not as solid as he once had been. Even before Smith spoke, I knew he was right, as I felt the line of Father's shoulders a little below mine.

"It's Sandy who is the taller — a modern-day Goliath!" Smith laughed at the expression on Father's face. "You should be proud, MacKay. Today your Sandy has proved himself to be a hard worker, as well as strong."

I smiled with pride to hear what Father said next. "I am, Ben. Without Sandy, the farm would have foundered while I was away. But time's wasting here and the Blue Team is pulling ahead, so I'll take their whisky to them and perhaps you can catch up."

We slogged through the rest of the afternoon and it was neck and neck between the Greens and Blues. When it was time for our last load of wood to be hauled, Angus and I came into the farmyard almost as one. I was tired now; he was, too. The rope on the sled bit into my chest, making the skin red and raw. Angus was sweating, his face strained and scarlet with exertion as he tried to match me, stride for stride. I forced my feet forward, concentrating on reaching the side of the barn first. The women had come to watch and our teammates ran alongside us, cheering and hooting in encouragement. I felt as if a dam broke inside me and a last flood of strength flowed into my legs. I surged forward. My sled went to the woodpile first. My cheering teammates rushed to stack the wood, but Uncle William's voice rang out proudly as he shouted, "I declare Green the winners! Each shall receive thirty shot as their prize. But one of their number, the one they think has contributed most, shall be called King of the Wood, and receive this fine powder horn as well."

Before I even had a chance to glance at the horn that Uncle William held above his head, my teammates began to chant as one, "Sandy! Sandy! Sandy!" and did not stop until Uncle William walked over to me and slung the horn over my shoulder. The others broke into loud huzzahs that made my face burn with both pride and embarrassment. I glanced quickly over at Father, wanting to see his expression, but he had bent down and was picking up Samuel, tickling him to make him laugh. All that evening as we feasted and danced,

I looked for an opportunity to talk with him, to ask once more if I could go with him and Angus should the militia be called out again. But Father was always in the thick of things, surrounded by others, laughing and enjoying himself as I had not seen him do for over a year.

Eventually I gave up and allowed myself to be swirled away to celebrate with my team, who kept plying me with whisky until I felt sick to my stomach and the world began to tilt around me.

Neither Father nor Mother were best pleased with me that night, or the next morning as I hung green-faced over my horse's neck when it came time to make our way home.

"We treat you like a man, and look what happens, Sandy! Like a greedy child, you don't know when to stop." Father's face was pinched with disgust. Those were the last words he spoke to me for several days.

* * *

By June, with Father's health on the mend, Morag was finally able to become a bride. She and Eric Holzer had been sweet on each other since they were little more than my age, always finding each other at any gatherings we had and sitting together when a travelling preacher came by. If the war had not come, they would have married a whole year ago.

I liked Eric well enough, or rather I had, until he had not accompanied the militia when they mustered. Instead, his father had bought men to take both their places, men who drifted off into the woods as the company marched towards Niagara and were never seen again, or so Angus told me.

I was surprised that Father would accept such a coward as a son-in-law, but when I said as much, his face hardened and he said, "Don't be so quick to judge, Sandy. Eric is the only child the Holzers have." I did not see what that had to do with anything, but held my tongue.

It was our turn for the preacher to hold the weekly service at our farm on the first Sunday in June, the 6th, and Eric and Morag would marry in front of our friends and neighbours. Then, at the end of the day's festivities, Morag would return with the Holzers to start her new life with them.

We were busy, with little time to be sad that Morag would leave us. Mother and the girls baked and cooked for days. Father made me, Angus and Drew build benches for the congregation to sit in the shade of our apple orchard rather than on the ground. It seemed a waste of effort, as we would only take them apart once the wedding was over and use them for firewood. Perhaps my judgement was clouded. I felt restless and angry that we were preparing for such a frivolous thing as a wedding when there were rumours that the Americans were planning to attack both from the lake and by marching up from Fort Niagara.

Only a month earlier, I had fumed when Angus had an actual encounter with the Americans. He and some of the other militia commanded by Captain Hatt had been guarding the King's Head Inn on Burlington Beach. Two American schooners had come and fired upon the militia to drive them off. I told Angus they should have stood their ground, which is what I would have done in his shoes. Angus just smiled and shook his head. That made me furious, for while our militia had skulked in the bushes, the American troops landed, ransacked the inn and burnt it to the ground. I would have expected them to stay and make this their base for further feints, but Angus said they were merely taunting us to show us what they could do.

Some said they were going to march on Burlington Heights, then York, and who knows where after that. Yet here we were doing *nothing* when Burlington Heights was less than an hour's ride away. I admit that it was an unworthy thought, but I hoped the Americans *would* invade. Then surely every man and boy would be called to defend our homes. I would be able to show Father and Angus just what I could do — and that would be to fight to the death, not run away and hide.

I dared not say anything to Father, but turned instead to Angus as we were carrying the finished benches out from the barn into the orchard. "Why are we doing *this* when an invasion might be taking place?"

Angus shrugged and gave me his slow smile. "They're just rumours, Sandy. The army fell back from Fort George to Burlington Heights and they've camped around Colonel Beasley's house to regroup. Ever since then, not a day has gone by without someone claiming that the whole American army is on its way to slaughter us all in our beds. It's nine days and we've not seen anything of them. They're not coming, I tell you. Our army will march back all the better for the rest and send the Yankees scurrying across the Niagara River again."

"But surely they'll call the militia out if there is any sign of them," I shot back. "How would it look if you got the call to muster tomorrow and half the congregation left the wedding and rode off?" I spat on the ground before continuing. "All except the groom, of course. He wouldn't go anywhere!"

Angus's smile wavered slightly. "Eric wanted to fight but he couldn't go against his father, just like we would never go against ours." As we positioned the last bench, Angus sat down, looking more sombre than I had ever seen him. "As to whether they'd call upon the militia, that remains to be seen. The British officers don't seem to have too high an opinion of us, despite what we did at Queenston. Given the choice, they keep us doing guard duty or labouring, not fighting to protect what is ours. They pay us pennies and keep us short of supplies and arms, so what do they expect?"

I was shocked to hear Angus speak this way and sank down on the bench next to him. "But you'd never not go, not if the call to muster came?"

"No, I'd go. Father and Mother have always brought us up to do our duty. Mother frets, I know, but she's proud, too. Only the other day when I set off to guard the inn, she got all misty-eyed and told me that I was the twin of Uncle Roger."

Angus was silent for a few seconds. I knew he was thinking of the uncle we had never met, the one whose story had been drummed into us. He had been Mother's brother as well as Father's best friend. And they'd fought for the British together, but Roger had been killed when he'd returned secretly to his old farm in New York State. He'd been bent on retrieving the silver he'd buried there — silver Mother's family could not carry when they first fled. And he'd been killed during a heated argument with people he had thought to be friends, not just neighbours; those people had taken the abandoned farm for themselves.

"We can't let the country that drove out our parents take over here!" Angus spoke quietly but with determination.

"Huzzah!" I shouted, relieved that his resolve was still firm. "Race you back to the house." I waited until Angus surged to his feet and took off running before I set after him. I still beat him and did not have to puff and wheeze, as he did.

I don't think that any of us expected to sleep well before the wedding. Morag and Polly were whispering long into the night in the room they shared with Ellen. This was no surprise, since Polly had never been without Morag's company and now would have only Ellen. I could hear the murmur of voices from Mother and Father's room, although I could not make out what they said. I could hear Samuel chattering to Drew in their small room. Only the room I shared with Angus was quiet, except for Angus's infernal snoring. I could not sleep for it, and my mind roiled with thoughts of what might happen if the American army did attack. I returned to my earlier thought, that age would be no barrier then — every able-bodied man or boy would be needed.

The heat that night did not help. It seemed that our weather was nothing but extremes this year — perhaps a reflection of our troubled times. Ice had remained in the creeks until mid-April and now we baked and boiled as if it were late summer rather than early June. I tossed and turned in my bed, trying to find a cooler spot on my pillow, but to no avail. I lost track of the hours I lay awake, but I didn't sleep until after I heard thunder in the distance, thunder that I hoped would bring a brief shower to cool us down but not spoil tomorrow's meeting and Morag's wedding.

When the brothers Hatt arrived with their families early the next morning, they brought exciting news. I would have set off immediately into the night had I known what last night's thunder really was — the sound of cannon! The American army had penetrated as far as Stoney Creek, a scant fifteen miles from where we were. But best of all was that our army had trounced them near the farms of the Gage brothers and sent those Yankees fleeing for their lives, and two of their generals had been taken!

During the hubbub at this news, I took Angus aside, out of Father's hearing. "We should go, you and I. From what Captain Hatt says, there are still Yankees lurking in the woods round Gages' farms. We can help flush them out. We won't be missed with so many here. Let's saddle the horses and go!"

At first Angus didn't reply, but I knew he was thinking about it because he got the wrinkle between his eyebrows that always comes when something concerns him. "No, Sandy. Men in fear of their lives are dangerous adversaries," he said. "They have nothing to lose and everything to gain." He gave me his broad grin, the one that melted many a girl's heart, and waved a hand towards the crowd now thronging our apple orchard. "Let's celebrate Morag's wedding and the fact that the pluck of our soldiers has given us the chance to do so."

I let him pull me along with him as he headed towards the crowd, but I was able to slip away when his attention was diverted by Callum Murdoch, now standing with only a stout cane rather than a crutch, holding hands with Amy Mason.

It took me just minutes to saddle Hamish and grab Angus's musket from the house. I had my own shot and powder. I thought of taking the time to change my clothes, but wanted to be on my way before anyone noticed that I was gone. I led the horse quietly away from the house until we reached the track to Wilson Street, and then on to the Iroquois trail towards Stoney Creek and the battlefield. Once I was safely out of earshot, I mounted as quickly as I could and urged Hamish to a gallop.

I swear that the whole of Ancaster was at our farm that morning, for I encountered no one as I rode through the village itself. I prayed that the presence of so many people at the wedding would conceal my absence just a little while. If my luck held, it might not even be noticed at all.

Once on the road, I was surprised to see my first Yankees. A more miserable set of men would be hard to find. They trudged along, their eyes down, faces pale, with little or no attempt at military order. Many people had turned out to savour their defeat and dejection — families in wagons, groups of men on horseback like me, all headed towards the battleground. I asked one man who rode alongside me why the Yankees were allowed such liberty. He shrugged, suggesting there might not be enough soldiers either to imprison them or pursue them. We jeered and catcalled. One lad rode his horse at a group of them and the Americans immediately panicked and attempted to run, although it was more of a stagger than anything.

Laughing at their terror, the lad did it again, but this time the Yankees were wise to him and did not scatter in panic. Most just went doggedly on, but one had enough of a spark of defiance to raise his fist and shake it at the boy, shouting, "Just you wait! We'll be back but with a bigger army!" He said more, but it was drowned out as we all shouted insults back.

The Gage farms were surrounded by thick forest and as I rode through it, I could hear voices and movement, causing me to wonder how many men still wandered or hid there. Captain Hatt had said that the British fell upon the American camp in the middle of the night, so it was likely there were still fugitives or strays in the woods.

I had never before been to visit the Gages, although I had heard Father talk of them, saying that they were carving out good farms from the forest. But good farms were not what I saw that day. Their crops had been flattened. All the rail fences dividing the fields had been torn down and trampled, in some cases shattered. The remains of campfires, some still smouldering, marked the ground like sores, their smoke mingling with the smell of powder that tainted the air. Abandoned guns and equipment were scattered thickly across the ground. Bodies lay where they had fallen, British and American intermingled. Many wounded spilled out from the farmhouse ahead of me, lying by its doorway or slumped against the wall. A woman, a small girl of about eight by her side, was offering them water from a dipper, which they took gratefully. People were moving around the field, some helping themselves to souvenirs, others truly helping by carrying the wounded to the house.

"Hey, you!" a voice called. One of the men tending to the wounded had stopped, raised a hand to his eyes to shield them from the sun and was looking in my direction. "Is that you, Angus MacKay?"

I understood the man's confusion. On horseback my size was less apparent, and we MacKays all had a look of our mother, with the same fairish hair, although mine was more a light brown to Angus's butter blond.

"No, sir," I replied, "I'm Angus's brother, Sandy, come to see the battle site."

He sighed, and then spat on the ground. "Tether

your horse and come make yourself useful rather than gawking."

I did as I was told, tying Hamish to the rail on the porch, and then loping back to the man.

In the time it took me, he had gathered a group of young men and was rattling out orders. Some men were from the Gage family itself. They were sent to get an ox sled. The others were militiamen. The man giving orders was, I learned, John Lee, a sergeant in the 5th Lincoln, who knew Father and Angus well. Our job, he told us, was to gather the dead and dig two graves, big enough to take them all — one by what was left of the church, the other by a knoll topped by an abandoned American gun. I did not know which was worse, the grave digging or the collecting, but it was the collecting to which I was assigned, along with another young fellow. As we were moving away, Sergeant Lee called me back. "You're MacKay's boy, yet you've not turned out to any militia training. Are you simple in the head or subject to fits? For there can be no other reason that MacKay would not have a son of his do his duty."

I bristled at his remarks, unhappy both at the suggestion that I was simple and that my Father had shirked his duty.

"Sir," I said, drawing myself to my full height, which I was happy to note allowed me to look down at Lee, "although I am big for my age, I do not turn fourteen until later this month. My father will not let me go to war until I am sixteen, as he values my work — the equal of any grown man's — while he and Angus are off soldiering!"

My partner sniggered at the look of shock on Lee's face. "He's a big 'un, isn't he?"

Lee smiled. "Yes, he is, Jack. Has a touch of his father's pride and bite, too." He turned back to me. "Let's see if your work is as valuable as your father thinks. If it is, you can teach my lazy rapscallion of a son some better ways. Off with you both, now."

Jack Lee was giggling fit to burst at his father's embarrassment, but his smile faded once we set to work, carrying the bodies over to the ox sled and loading them onto it.

I had seen the dead once before. We had all been present when Uncle William's wife had died of a raging fever. When it was over, Aunt Mary had looked like a peaceful shadow of herself, one that you could almost think asleep rather than dead.

The dead here were different. They lay twisted, their bodies cratered with shot, flies clustering around their wounds. Some had faces contorted in terror. Others looked surprised at what had befallen them. They stank of blood, piss and shit.

They all felt heavy, leaking fluids as we moved them.

I felt my gorge rising and swallowed hard. Jack was faring no better. His face was greenish, his brow dotted with sweat. He was slighter than I was, but my strength allowed us to work fast. That was good. Although neither of us said so, I knew that we both wanted this job done quickly.

I lost count of how many bodies we moved — thirty, forty, fifty. When Jack's father gave us leave to wash up, I poured an icy bucket of water over my head. Jack copied me and we sat down under the shade of a tree, letting the water cool us.

"It doesn't get rid of the stench, but that felt good." Jack looked sideways at me as he spoke. "I have a year in age on you, so I'll go next time the militia are called out, but after seeing this, let us hope the Americans have learned their lesson and the war will end." He was breathing hard. Without warning he doubled over and vomited on the ground.

I jumped to my feet to escape the splatter. He rose quickly, too. "It's the stink," he said. "I'm not afraid, truly I'm not." His eyes glittered in the shadows as he looked at me.

"I know that," I said. "I know that you're not scared."

My words heartened him and his ready grin flickered across his face. "Old Fuss," he said, indicating his father over by one of pits, "will be quick to find us more work if he spots us with idle hands. Let's head into the woods to see what we can find there. Billy Green came back with a full ammunition pouch, and even an officer's sword. Wouldn't we be the swells if we found treasure like that?"

It did not take me long to agree. By the sun, it was after noon, and I would soon have to ride for home. But when I spotted a column of redcoats marching out of the forest, obviously come from Burlington Heights, it decided me. I nodded. Let them do what work remained!

Jack was a chatterbox. As we made our way into the trees he had me laughing at the outrageous stories he told, most of which involved him finding ways to get out of his chores and go off exploring and hunting in the woods.

This made me think on what might await me should Father discover my absence. I wondered whether I should ride for home right then.

"What's wrong?" Jack asked, looking closely at me.

I confessed that I had come without permission, sneaking off from my sister's wedding celebrations, and that I dreaded facing my father's anger when I returned. I did not add that this was the first time ever that I had done something I knew Father would have forbidden.

Jack laughed. "So you get a beating, but the pain of a beating fades fast and is soon forgotten. Anyway, your father wouldn't dare take a switch to someone your size."

His words set off a twinge of guilt, for no matter how badly we behaved, it was rare that Father beat us. I could only recall one time, when I had deliberately run away from Drew in the forest, and it had taken Father and Angus the good part of a day and night to find him. Father had cut a switch, laid me over his knee and whacked me until Mother caught his arm to stop him. Father cuffed us occasionally to show his displeasure, but beat us regularly, no. I feared his disapproving silence far more than his hands.

My thoughts were cut short as Jack froze.

He whispered, "Did you hear that?"

I listened, straining my ears to hear what he had. There was nothing at first, then the rustling of leaves as someone or something moved close by. I cursed myself, for I had left Angus's musket strapped to my saddle. Putting my finger to my lips, I moved as quietly as I could in the direction of the noise, using my other hand to signal Jack to follow me.

The noise came again, and I forced myself through the undergrowth and burst into a clearing, Jack treading on my heels in his eagerness to follow. We were confronted by a Yankee soldier. He was just lowering himself onto the ground, his back against a tree, but sprang to his feet as soon as he saw us.

I rushed him, sending him crashing back against the tree. He fought hard, wriggling to push me off. He was smaller than me, but wiry and strong. One hand was reaching to his side, and I realised that he was trying to grab the bayonet that was lying alongside his musket. I dared not take my attention from him, but I sensed rather than saw Jack dancing round helplessly, aiming the odd kick at the man, but more often getting me with his foot.

"Jack," I bellowed, "grab the bayonet and musket."

Jack snatched up both. Once that danger had passed, it was as if all fight left the American. He lay there limp on the ground, not even moving when I stood up.

"Get up, you bastard," I snarled, and Jack prodded him with the bayonet when he did not move quickly enough for his liking.

"Boys, boys," the man said, now on his feet, "don't be hasty." He held his hands out from his body, showing us the palms. "I'll not give you trouble. I've been hiding in this godforsaken forest waiting for the redcoats to leave. All I want is to get away, find my regiment and get back home." He smiled then, a nervous smile that went as quickly as it came. "I'm not a real soldier, just a farmer like your fathers, I'd reckon. I've got little ones at home. Why not pretend you've not seen me?" As he spoke, I realised he was edging away from us. Before he could try to flee, I darted forward, grabbed his arm and twisted it behind his back, hard.

He squealed, and then muttered, "Easy, easy," but I wasn't in the mood to be easy. Whether he had children or not did not concern me, or that he was a farmer. He had left them behind and come north to take our farms from *us*, and leave children *here* fatherless. I pushed his arm up higher, enjoying the way he rose on his toes to lessen the pain.

"Come on, Jack," I said, "let's take this piece of dung back and hand him over to the redcoats." Jack laughed when I added, "You waited too long, see. Our soldiers left, but they've come back now just to round up scum like you!"

When we came out of the forest, pushing our prisoner ahead of us, a cry went up. Jack's father called us both "bully boys" and said how proud we had made him and that he would be sure to tell my father that when next he saw him. Other prisoners had been rounded up and we happily handed ours over. We didn't mention the weapons we had taken from him. Jack kept the bayonet and I took the musket, thinking that this at least would please Father.

All my euphoria leached away on my ride home. As dusk descended I knew there was no hope that my absence had gone unnoticed. A foolish shred of hope that Father would applaud my daring was all I had, but deep in my heart I knew that this would not be so.

I was not wrong.

Father was sitting on the porch as I rode in, Angus by his side. Mother must have been listening for the sound of Hamish's hooves because she immediately appeared in the doorway, her face white and her eyes red. I wanted to throw myself down from my horse and rush to tell her how sorry I was for causing her such worry, but I knew I had to face Father first. Without looking around, Father said, "Hannah, go inside. I will speak to Alexander."

Mother hesitated slightly, but turned and without a word to him or to me quietly closed the door behind her.

Father remained motionless in his chair, sitting very erect, a hand resting on each knee. I wondered whether he feared that he might explode with anger should he move but an inch.

Angus rushed over, ready to take Hamish away to the stables. Moving around the other side of Hamish where Father could not see, he whispered, "I couldn't cover your absence when Father asked where you were, Sandy. Someone said they'd seen you leading Hamish away. Father kept it from Mother for as long as he could, but when the Holzers and Morag made ready to go, she wanted the whole family to wave them off, and Father had to tell her that you had run off, likely heading for the site of the battle. He's angry, Sandy, angrier than I've ever seen him."

Carrying a musket in each hand, I took a deep breath and walked up the steps to Father. He stood up from his seat and looked steadily at me. Our eyes met and I stiffened my spine, readying myself for what was to come.

"Father, I'm sorry I went without permission, but I knew that if I asked, you would say no. I wanted to go to where they fought, to do something other than work on the farm, maybe help track down some Yankees . . . "

I was conscious that my excuse sounded feeble and whining, that my words could not convey the need to act that burned inside me each and every day. Would he ever understand the feeling I had that this was what I was meant to do, that unless I did something now, this war — my one chance for excitement and meaning — would end before I did anything.

Father continued staring at me, the muscles in his jaw working as if he were chewing.

"I was a help, I swear," I went on. "You can ask John Lee. He was there. I worked with him and others. We cleared the battlefield of dead. Buried them. Then his son and I, we caught a Yankee soldier hiding in the woods. This is his musket. Mr. Lee said I was a bully boy, a boy to be proud of, and that he would tell you so when he saw you." I had no more words, not in the face of my father's flat stare and silence. All I could do was stand there and see what he would do.

Father's voice when he finally spoke was quiet, each word distinct, clipped as if he resented its loss. "Your mother has spent the last few hours of what should have been a happy day weeping, certain that her son had been killed through his own foolhardiness. Your sister left this house without the joy and celebration of her marriage that were her due. You took what was not yours to take, something we can ill afford to replace. You value your own life and safety lightly, willing to exchange them for an adventure and vainglory. I thought I had raised you better. I am ashamed of you, Alexander."

Father stared hard at me. His words felt as if they etched themselves with acid on my skin, burning deep.

I could not meet his eyes. I stared down at my feet, staying like that even as I heard him turn and walk into the house, closing the door quietly but firmly behind him.

I did not look up, not even when Angus was at my side, a hand placed on my shoulder. I did not want him to see the tears that ran down my face. Without speaking, he led me into the house. All was dark, save for a candle left burning on the table to light us to our room. I heard the murmur of voices from my parents' room. Drew popped his head round the door of the room he shared with Samuel, his eyes wide with excitement, but quickly withdrew when Angus waved him off.

I threw myself on my bed and turned my face to the wall. I knew that I had been at fault, but my soul was wounded by Father's coldness towards me.

"Sandy — " Angus's voice was low. "Why did you go? Surely you knew what Father's reaction would be."

I rolled onto my back and stared at the ceiling. "I knew it was wrong, but I thought he would be proud that I wanted to do something, that I showed spirit." I paused and thought of the smile on John Lee's face when he had seen Jack and me with our prisoner, and how I had felt when he praised me. "Any other man would have been."

"It's your spirit that frightens him, Sandy," Angus whispered.

"I don't see how, Angus," I said bitterly.

"It was spirit and daring like yours that got Uncle Roger killed," Angus said. "You know from Father's stories that he was the wild one, the one who acted first."

I didn't say anything, just felt fury building inside me, forcing out the sadness I had felt at Father's cold anger.

"There's guilt, too," Angus added. "Roger asked Father to go with him, but he dismissed the idea of going home to retrieve their money as foolhardy. He never dreamed that Roger would go alone and be killed."

"But I am not Roger!" My voice was loud, but I did not care.

He sighed. "When Father looks at you, I know that he sees Roger. He wants to keep you safe, as he could not do for Roger. He worries, too, that should anything happen to you, it would be the end of Mother."

I turned and looked at him in surprise.

Angus shrugged. "Even though she would deny it, you are her favourite, resembling Uncle Roger as you do."

I heard Angus's words and thought on them for much of that night. Although he had not intended to harden my resolve, he did, for my sadness and contrition curdled into anger that I should be forced to live my life in constraints because of a man who had been dead for more than twenty years. Somehow I would break free and convince Father and Mother that I was my own man, not the shadow of another. Words would not do it — only actions would count. Had I not shown them today that I was capable of handling myself well, and that no harm had come to me?

* * *

For most of that long summer Father didn't speak to me at all. I could have been a ghost in his house for all the direct attention he paid to me. A ghost who was still expected to provide labour, but one who was never spoken to and whose questions were answered only through a third person.

I know that Mother spoke to Father about it. I overheard snippets of conversations, but nothing she said — that I had learned my lesson, that this silent treatment had gone on long enough — moved him. Father had a reputation for being stubborn and hard-headed, but these were qualities he had passed on to me, too. I vowed that I would not break before he did. I did as I was told, worked harder even, as I wanted to give Father no further cause for complaint. I took my lead from him, and if I needed further instructions I would ask Angus, who then asked Father. Whatever reply was given, I acted upon it immediately, seeing no point in pretending that Angus needed to say it again for me.

This rift, this silence, cast a pall over what should have been a happy time for us. With the Yankees driven back it was a period of relative peace and, strangely enough for a time of war, a time of new prosperity for the MacKay family.

The British now made their headquarters at Burlington Bay and they needed supplies and labour. Through Father's connections with the Hatts he was able to secure a contract to supply eggs to them and we doubled our production. Polly, aided by a willing Ellen, was in charge of our little industry, tending to more hens than I dreamed we could manage. Unusually, Ma seemed little interested, leaving much of the garden work to Polly. As that hot summer progressed, she spent more and more time just sitting on the porch mending or knitting. If I were nearby I would be aware that she was looking at me and, more often than not, she would sigh, causing me considerable guilt, for I feared that my strained relations with Father were the cause of her despondency. One hot morning in August I voiced my concern to Angus as he and I were clearing land, while Father had driven with Drew to Burlington Bay.

Angus started to laugh. "Alexander MacKay, around whom the earth revolves, the be all and end all of everything!" He shook his head. "Mother's not happy, that's for sure, but you're a gowk if you've not realised that we have another brother or sister on the way."

"When?" I stuttered.

"It's not something that has been talked about, Sandy, but I would say in a few months' time." He smiled and added, "Which is good, because then our little brother or sister will be older than Morag and Eric's child, its niece or nephew, if only by half a year or so."

"Morag, too!"

"Now *that* you can be forgiven for not knowing, Sandy. I only know because I overheard Mother telling Father after seeing Morag and Eric at last Sunday's meeting." Angus smiled. "It will be nice to have a new baby around the house again. Maybe it will lift the mood and you and Father can forget your differences."

Angus looked so happy that I did not wish to dash his hopes, so I just nodded as if I agreed.

* * *

As it turned out, the new baby did change things, but not in the way that Angus had hoped.

About three weeks later, Angus was taking the wagon with its crates of eggs to the army camp. Drew and Father were in the barn while I was mending the fence around our vegetable patch. Some soldiers billeted in the village had come creeping in the night to steal from us. They were drunk, paying little attention to what they trampled on. Their racket had woken the whole house, and all it took to send them away with their tails between their legs was Angus, Father and I to run at them brandishing stout sticks.

I was lost in my thoughts as we worked, but being nearer the house, I was the one who first heard Polly's screams, which were closely followed by Ellen flying out of the house, yelling as loudly as she could for Father to come quick. I set off running towards the house with Father scant seconds behind me.

Polly stood in the doorway. "The baby's coming, Father." She was white-faced, her eyes round, "I don't know what to do. Mother seems in such pain."

Father turned to me. "Sandy, take Hamish and ride for the village, but stop off on the way and ask Mrs. Brown to come over to help your mother. Find Dr. Tiffany if you can."

I had Hamish saddled before I realised that for the first time in months, Father had spoken directly to me.

The Browns' farmstead was only ten minutes' ride away. Even as I explained what was happening, Agatha Brown was gathering things together to take with her. She had five children of her own and I knew that her experience would calm Polly, who seemed all in a tizzy.

"Sandy," she said, "do your best to find the doctor. Your mother's not as young as she was, and there have been other babies lost." I gaped at her, surprised that she knew this. "Stop fly catching, Sandy, and get moving." Her words were harsh, but the smile accompanying them was gentle.

I leapt onto Hamish's back and rode as fast I could for the village, but my hopes were dashed even before I dismounted, as I saw a note pinned to Dr. Tiffany's door. That meant only one thing

— that he had been called out and could be as far away as Niagara. The note had been written that morning and said that the doctor was gone to Brantford and not likely to be home until tomorrow. I used the pencil hanging on a string from the door to write on his note that he should come to the MacKays' as soon as he could, but seeing that there was already another note above mine, I held out little hope that he would come in time. As I rode home I prayed that all would be well, that Mrs. Brown would have taken charge.

A sorry sight awaited me as I rode in to our farmyard. Drew and Ellen sat on the porch, little Samuel between them. Their heads were down and even though it was obvious she had been crying, Ellen was attempting to amuse Samuel by drawing patterns in the dirt with a stick. Even before I dismounted, I could hear Mother's moans and shrieks.

Ellen was on her feet and at my side in an instant. "Is he coming? Did you find the doctor?"

When I told her that he was away, her face crumpled and she began to cry in earnest, gulping sobs that quickly set Samuel off, too. I quickly tethered Hamish to the porch rail and scooped my little brother up into my arms, patting his back and whispering that he should be a brave boy if he could. Drew was up and had put his arms around Ellen, who buried her face into his shoulder. "It's been bad, Sandy," he said. "Mrs. Brown is there with Polly, but we don't know what's happening. Mother sounds as if she's hurting something terrible."

Drew's normally cheerful face was solemn. I put a hand on his shoulder. "Where's Father?"

"In the parlour. He told us to stay out here and watch Samuel."

"Is Angus not back yet?" I asked.

"Not yet."

"Here," I said, "take Samuel then. See if you can rock him to sleep."

Father was sitting in the rocking chair by the hearth, his head in his hands. He looked up as I came in, sighing when he saw that I was alone.

"Dr. Tiffany is away and likely not back today," I said. It felt strange to be speaking directly to Father.

"I feared that," Father said. "Your Aunt Mary helped birth all of you, but with her gone, Mrs. Brown is a good substitute."

I felt awkward standing there, and half turned to rejoin the younger ones outside, but with a gesture Father halted me.

"Sit with me, Sandy," he said.

I took the seat opposite him. My hands clenched into fists each time Mother moaned or cried out.

Father's hands gripped the arms of his rocking chair, his knuckles white. Mrs. Brown's voice was a murmur, gentle and soothing.

"Each child is a gift." Father's voice was low, so low that I was not sure he was talking to me at all, but rather just saying his thoughts out loud. Then he addressed me directly. "Both your mother and I love you all dearly. Never forget that."

I think that Father would have said more, but Mother screamed so loudly that he leaped up from his chair. He stood there for what seemed like minutes, as if undecided what to do. Mother's moans had turned to sobs and even before Mrs. Brown appeared in the bedroom door, I knew that things had gone awry.

Her face was red and beaded with sweat. "I'm sorry, Rob, the baby was stillborn. It was a hard birthing and Hannah is weakened by it. You should be by her side now."

At Mrs. Brown's words Father crumpled in on himself and staggered as if he would fall. I moved to his side, placing an arm around his waist to steady him. For one brief moment, he leaned against me, then straightened his shoulders and went with Mrs. Brown.

I waited there, not sure what to do, whether to go and tell the younger ones, or to wait to see if

Father needed me again. In the end, I decided that it was not fair to leave the younger ones worrying, especially since Mother no longer cried out and they might think she had died. All three were crying and their tears unmanned me, too, so that I could no longer hold back the sobs that had filled me up. There had been other babies who had died, but it was not spoken of, and when we were younger I suppose we were less aware.

We were sitting on the porch steps in a huddle when Father came out to find me.

His face was grey. He stood looking down at us before he spoke. "Your mother is tired but she will be fine. Drew and Ellen, take Samuel inside and help Polly prepare some food. If Mrs. Brown sees fit, you may visit with your mother briefly." There was another pause, then Father said, "Sandy, I need you to come with me."

I followed him to the barn, where he handed me a spade. "Go dig a grave, Sandy, on the bank overlooking the creek." Father's voice cracked and he stumbled over his next words. "It doesn't have to be big, but make it deep so that critters will not dig it up. Perhaps to the side of the willow. I will come and join you there when I'm ready."

It did not take me long at all to do as Father asked. As I was digging, I realised that there were three other small mounds beneath the trees. I felt stupid that I had never noticed them before. I even had time to gather stones from the creek bank to either build a cairn over the grave or just to put on top, but still Father did not come. I went back up to the farm, willing to risk his anger that I had disobeyed him again.

I found him sitting on a milking stool at the far end of the barn, in the shadows. A small, crudely built coffin was laid across his knees, its lid propped up against the wall behind. Around his feet were curls of pale wood shavings.

The grim expression on his face as he looked down at the tiny coffin softened slightly. "Ah, Sandy, you came looking for me. I was hoping that Angus would return and that he could do what I cannot. I wanted to spare you if I could."

I was puzzled. "I can do what needs to be done, sir. Just tell me what it is."

"You need to get your brother for me."

"But Angus is not here," I said, puzzled. "And why would you need Drew when you have me?"

Father closed his eyes and when he spoke, his words were so faint that I had to strain to hear them. "Your newest brother, Sandy. I am sorry, but I find myself unable to do this." His voice steadied. Tears were running unchecked down his face but he seemed unaware of them. "Go to Mrs. Brown, who will know what to do. Make sure that the younger ones don't see. Bring him to me and then we will bury him."

I tapped gently on the bedroom door. Mrs. Brown opened it just a crack. When I told her what Father wanted she nodded and told me to meet her at the back of the house. I didn't have to wait long before she appeared, and silently passed my brother's body to me. I held him gently, thinking of the times I had held Samuel when he was newborn. The weight and feel were the same and my arms remembered how to hold a baby, but this baby was cold. Mrs. Brown had covered his face with the shawl. With one finger, I eased it aside. He was beautiful, like a little doll carved out of white wood. His eyes were closed and I marvelled at the delicate veins I saw on his eyelids — like petals. A tuft of fiery red hair pushed out from beneath the shawl. Gently, I covered his face again and started on the long walk to where Father waited.

Father stood up as I entered the barn. He held out the coffin to me. I carefully laid my brother into it, tucking the shawl around him. It was foolish, but I did not want the rough sides to touch him.

Father had a look of such pain on his face that I almost could not bear to look at him. "Let me do this," I said. "You go to Mother and the others."

He hesitated, but I gently took the coffin from him. "I can do this for you."

Father dashed away tears with the back of his hand. "You are a good boy, Sandy," he said, his voice thick.

I did not pick up the tiny lid and nail it down until he had gone into the house. It was only after I shovelled dirt down onto the coffin and knelt beneath the willow to place a coverlet of stones upon the grave that I realised I did not know my brother's name. I didn't even know whether he had been given one. I wondered if, had he lived, they would have called him Roger.

Chapter 4
December 1813

It seemed for all the rest of that year as if we were a family holding our breath, on edge in case something should disturb our fragile tranquility. Neither Mother nor Father spoke of the dead baby and all of us followed their lead. Mother was soon up and running the household again, with Polly as her trusty lieutenant, and if she was more prone to temper than before, no one remarked upon it.

Father did not acknowledge that the silence between him and me had been broken, nor indeed that there had ever been one. He now spoke to me as much as he did the others, which was little, as a thoughtful silence was his preferred state. Quite often, at the end of the day's labours, before the light failed and we went in to eat, he would bundle up and walk down to the creek. Mother never went there.

Father seemed to find Angus the most restful company. Angus had never been a great talker, never full of questions like I was, but just happy in himself and his work. I tried to be like him, but it was hard, and I recognised that I was a disturbance to Father. He took to keeping Angus working alongside him and sent me on those errands to the army camp or the mill that had previously been Angus's domain.

Although it saddened me that Father was not easy in my company, I did not complain, for I had a freedom that had been lacking, a freedom to escape the confines of our farm, to learn more of the world and to be treated as less of a child, my size fooling many of my newfound acquaintances. No time limits were set on me. If there was a particular job that required my labour, then I had to return with all speed, but if not, then as long as I returned before night fell, nothing was said.

I became something of a favourite at the army camp, perhaps because I was always eager to listen to the soldiers' tall tales. It was there, too, that I could now gather news of how the war went. I was careful though to tell only Father and Angus, letting Father decide what he would tell the others. I thought he was wrong to shield Mother and the girls, because they would hear it at our Sunday meetings and by then, through the telling and imaginings of others, it all sounded so much worse.

Mother was almost hysterical when she heard

of the dreadful events at Newark at the start of December, although she held back her tears and wails until we returned home. "Rob," she cried, "they burned the village. They turned out women, children, old men and even those sick in their beds into the snow. How can they be so cruel?"

Father drew her close and wiped away her tears. "Hannah," he said, "war drives men mad."

"But, what's to stop them advancing further?" Mother wailed. "And they were saying that Abraham Markle from our *own* village was there with Joseph Willcocks, leading the renegades, those so-called Canadian Volunteers."

Father's face hardened. "I had little good to say about Markle when he was here, Hannah, and now he has confirmed my ill opinion of him. The British will not let this atrocity go unpunished. You'll see."

Mother's tears ceased but worry was still clear on her face.

Father patted her hand. "With winter coming, there will be little troop movement, so don't fret that we will be in danger here."

Mother seemed mollified, but then said, "But what about my father, Rob — his smithy is so close to the border." She looked set to cry anew, but Father soothed her worries, telling her that her father was a seasoned veteran who would survive such troubled times.

I did not share his confidence and wished that the Lincolns would muster and march so I could press my case to go with them once more. Father was right, though. When I was at the camp, I heard news of the retaliation. I only told Mother that Fort George had been recaptured. I did not tell her that British troops had crossed the border and burned American villages. I also heard, but remained silent about, the capture of Fort Niagara on the American side of the river, and that the men of the area, the 1st Lincoln militia, had been in the thick of it, piloting the bateaux, and then fighting alongside the British. I am sure that they were as eager as I would have been to get revenge for Newark, for most came from that area.

* * *

When spring came in 1814, it marked the start of an exciting time. On several occasions Father even allowed me to work as a day labourer at the camp on Burlington Heights if I was not needed at home, letting me keep the money I earned — a whole two shillings.

I counted myself very fortunate, and since the militia mustered only to drill, my feelings of resentment lessened. I was determined that if Angus and Father were mustered again, this time I would *not* be left behind.

I also became an uncle. Morag had a baby girl whom she called Hannah after our mother. The baby was a pretty thing, but I could not help thinking that her birth would give Eric yet another reason why he could shirk his duty, something that were I in his place, I would *never* do.

One of the biggest events was the Assizes. Ancaster was proud to be chosen for such an event. We all thrilled to think that traitors were coming before the magistrates and would now get the punishment they deserved for their treachery.

The MacKays had always been proud to be Loyalists. It was why my parents had left their home in New York's Mohawk Valley, moved to Upper Canada and cast our lot with the British. But, sadly, there were others who could not be trusted. They took free land grants from the Crown, but still harboured American sympathies deep in their hearts. Father said little about such men, but we always took our grain to the Hatt brothers' Red Mill, rather than the Union Mill, even though the Union was closer. Father had no regard for one of its owners, the infamous Abraham Markle who had behaved so despicably at Newark. It was no surprise that his name was amongst the many who had been arraigned for treason and would be tried *in absentia* at the Assizes. Van Camp's name was on the list too. I wondered where he had fled, and whether his family had gone, too.

I had never seen nor heard of an event of such importance in all my days. The chief justice of Canada was to preside as judge, along with two others who had come from York itself. Our own magistrates, the Hatt brothers, were to assist. Ancaster was awash with visitors, and many families made money by giving them board and lodging. Grandfather Livesay travelled from his forge near Niagara to stay with us so he could attend the trials. He, like my father, was staunch in his views and wanted to see justice done. Living close to the border, he had probably seen more than his fair share of traitorous behaviour.

For us all, Grandfather's visit was a blessing. Mother seemed cheerful for the first time in many months. We all knew she hoped he would choose to stay and end his days among us, as he had no family left but her. He had lived for nearly twenty years by the great Falls, where he had set up his smithy after leaving Butler's Rangers. He had been Father's sergeant through the long years fighting the American Revolution. Grandfather talked fondly of his home there, so I was not sure that Mother's wish would come about. For the rest of us, we had time to get to know our grandfather, whom we saw only rarely. He was a man quick to laugh and joke — things which had been lacking in our house for many months.

I burned to attend the trials, to see the great men of our colony dispense justice, but thought it unlikely that I would be allowed. I was astonished when my grandfather asked me to accompany him, saying that a clever young fellow like myself could learn from such an event. I was even more surprised when Father agreed.

I expected the Assizes to be exciting, but after just a few days I was bored by their tedium. The accused were a sorry lot, corrupt and self-serving, save for one older man who seemed confused and ill-used. Although many were arraigned, only nineteen had been caught. The biggest traitors, those who actually fought against their own country, Markle and Joseph Willcocks — the worst blackguard of all — were safely with their American friends, cocking a snook at us and laughing.

What did inspire me was the prosecutor, John Beverley Robinson. I had thought that the attorney general of Upper Canada would be a man at least my father's age, if not my grandfather's, but he was so young a man, he looked as if he had just started shaving. Yet he had served at both Detroit and Queenston — just like Father and Angus — and he spoke with an authority that made men much older hang on his every word.

Grandfather was impressed, too, and told me that I should watch Robinson closely and learn from him. When the Assizes finally ended I felt a curious mixture of feelings. I had a great satisfaction that justice had been done to some measure, with fourteen of the accused being found guilty. I was sad that although some were granted clemency, the old man was not one of them. I thought that he was gullible and had been tricked by others.

I shuddered when Chief Justice Scott read out the sentence that those found guilty were to be hung, drawn and quartered before being beheaded. No man with any sense would risk such punishment, and I hoped that those still among us who were less than loyal would take note.

The proceedings had been so dull that I was surprised to find myself eager to get back to my duties on the farm. I knew that my future would not be there, as Angus would inherit the land, but Father had talked about getting more land for "his boys." If he did that, then it could all go to Drew and Samuel, as far as I was concerned. Drew had changed in the years of the war, and it was clear that he loved the land as much as Father and Angus did. I would make another life for myself. Before the Assizes I had thought that, if money could be found for my studies, law might be the job for me, but with it so deadly dull, I now knew I would have to find something else.

Grandfather left us soon after the verdicts were announced in the middle of June. We were all sad to see him leave, but happy that Mother had prevailed upon him to close up his smithy, which he would do at the end of the summer, and return to live with us before winter. This news buoyed us up, but rumours were again flying that American troops were massing on their side of the Niagara River. These rumours led to action, with the militia drilling and Father and Angus being called to Burlington Heights to labour there for days at a time.

Now that relations between Father and me were restored, I vowed that I would not go against his wishes, but still I had to ask that I might go, too. I chose my time well, waiting until he and Angus returned after four days' hard labour cutting brush, and with the knowledge that they had only a night at home until they had to return. Father looked weary, although he and Angus both tucked heartily into the stew Mother had prepared.

"Father, is it true that there will be an invasion?" Drew asked.

I could have hugged him and swung him around for asking.

"It would seem so." Father's concentration on his food was so great that he seemed to answer without thinking. It was only Mother's gasp that made him realise what he had said. "Hannah, Hannah, do not fret. Troops are already on the move to prevent any such incursion." He grimaced. "That is why they call on us to do the menial work around camp. We are due back tomorrow, and you must prepare yourself, Hannah, for Hatt has told me that the militia will march for the border eventually, too."

"Oh, Rob, could not someone else go? You and Angus are always the first to answer the call to duty." Mother's anguished words gave me the opening I needed.

"I could take your place tomorrow, Father, and you could stay here and set things in order for when you depart." I was holding my breath, thinking that if he agreed to this, then perhaps when the Lincolns did march he would let me go, too.

Father was silent for what seemed minutes. "Aye, all right, Sandy."

I knew better than to crow over my triumph, but made sure that Angus and I were up at dawn to make the journey to Burlington Heights. It was then that I learned what had led to my wish being granted. Three soldiers of the 103rd Foot had been flogged for abandoning their posts to go drinking at the inn. The whole camp, militia and all, had been forced to watch the punishment. Angus said that two had borne the whipping manfully, gritting their teeth and trying not to cry out as their backs were cut to bloody stripes, but one — a raw recruit, or so Father had described him to Angus — had wailed and screamed as each blow landed until finally he had lapsed into a merciful stupor. Even the most hardened men were green, seeing the state of his back.

"I vomited," Angus confessed. "Father did not, but he turned aside and could not watch. He's reluctant to be at the camp again, lest there be another flogging."

"Do you think there could be?" I asked.

"Perhaps," Angus said. "News of invasion and our orders to march might come any day. It makes the men tense, so discipline is tight."

As it happened, our day of labour was uneventful and we were dismissed until further notice. John Lee, who had praised me on the day of Morag's wedding, made much of me, telling Angus what a help I had been to him at Stoney Creek and how I was even more of a giant now than I had been then. I was flattered that he remembered me after more than a year, and hoped he had said similar things to Father. That might persuade him to let me go along when he and Angus marched with the militia.

Chapter 5
July 1814

We did not have long to wait for those orders. News came in early July that the Americans had crossed the river and that Fort Erie had fallen to them. Then came more news, of a battle at Chippawa Creek, where the Americans had bested our forces. Details were scarce, but by eavesdropping on Father and Angus I realised that it was something of a rout, with the Americans surprising our men and then forcing them to retreat. There were many casualties. I had to sneak around to hear this because Father tried to keep as much as he could from Mother, who now seemed to quail and cry at any news of the war. She was almost hysterical when he told her in the mildest terms that the Yankees had crossed the border, and he did not mention Chippawa at all. He tried to jolly her along with bluster, telling her that those Yankees would soon be sent home to lick their wounds once the British and militia marched down to meet them. I could feel a nervous excitement building, for surely now with the war coming so close and invasion being spoken of, Father would have to let me go with him.

I knew why Father was so sparing in his telling, for if Mother knew that the Americans had scouting parties riding where they chose in the area around the great Falls, she would fear for our grandfather's safety as well as worrying when the militia would actually march. Some said the Americans had come as far as Twenty Mile Creek, which was so close to us we dared not let her know such details.

On the ninth of July the 5th Lincoln marched — Father and Angus among them — but they marched without me, to my great sorrow and frustration. The arguments I used had not worked on Father before, and they did not work this time. He would not be moved. I argued furiously. I tried not to bluster, and was determined not to cry, presenting my arguments as logically as I could. It was all to no avail. I was to stay and work the farm with Drew.

I chafed at this decision. I worked and brooded. I knew that I was the equal if not the better in strength of many men, either militia or our army — some of the British soldiers were scrawny little men. Father's careful teaching had ensured that I was a better shot than most. I knew that I would be of use. Had I not already shown that? All that kept me from disobeying and following the militia was the memory of Father's silent anger. I was not sure I could endure that again.

My trips to deliver eggs to the army encampment were the only bright spots in an otherwise miserable existence, although I grew increasingly frustrated as I saw more and more troops moving south. I did at least get news of what was happening, news that the Lincolns were with the British army near the Falls, waiting to see what the Americans would do next.

Those found guilty at our Assizes were to be executed at Burlington Heights on July 20 and I made sure I would be there that day. I found myself having to play Father's role with Drew, who was desperate to come, too. He begged and pleaded, but I refused to listen.

When I arrived it seemed that almost everyone had turned out to witness the hangings. Families had driven out in wagons. Children wound through the feet of the people gathered near the makeshift gallows. Enterprising women were hawking pies and pastries they had made. Whisky and beer were to be had. The mood was excited and wild. I could feel my own anger swelling within me and soon I was shouting and cheering with the best of them.

I recognised many familiar faces in the crowd. Captain Hatt was there, perhaps in his role as magistrate, for he stood on a wagon bed with some British officers and John Beverley Robinson and Thomas Scott, the chief justice, to have a clearer view. A hand clapped me on the shoulder, and when I turned I saw the grinning face of my brother-in-law Eric.

I scanned the crowd behind us. "Surely you have not brought Morag and the baby here!" I exclaimed.

He laughed. "No, Sandy. Just my father and I came, but I have lost him in this crush." His breath was hot on my face, stinking of whisky. "What a spectacle this is going to be, seeing traitors get what they deserve. We shall tell our grandchildren of this day, you can be sure of that."

I bit back the reply that leaped into my mind that sometimes one could be a traitor through inaction just as much as action. How could Eric gloat when he had not done his duty and gone with the militia? I tried to move away from him, but he clung to my arm.

"Did you bring your wagon today or come on Hamish?" he asked. "If you've your wagon, then we can stand on it, like those bigwigs, and get a better view, too."

When I admitted that my wagon was under the trees, he pulled at me until I reluctantly led him to it, only to find others already using it.

Eric was all for throwing them off, but I refused. There was room for us still, and it was not his place to decide who might use it.

The sound of fifes and drums cut through the crowd's hubbub, which gradually died away as a grim procession made its way towards where we stood. The eight prisoners were bound and shackled, loaded in two wagons that were being led towards the trees. Nooses already hung around their necks, ready to be attached to wooden braces that had been constructed. I could not help but look for the old man. Unlike the others who were standing, albeit some were shaking, he was crouched down in the bed of the wagon, weeping. A woman I presumed to be his wife walked alongside. The wagon's slow pace enabled her to hold his hand, which she raised to her lips and kissed. Another man — not one of the prisoners, for he had no noose around his neck — knelt beside the old man, reading from a bible.

The crowd remained silent. The drummers and fifers halted and marched smartly to one side as the wagons were carefully positioned underneath the wooden gallows. A bugle was blown and John Beverley Robinson raised his voice to bellow out the sentence that had been passed. Even in the silence, I struggled to hear all that he said:

" . . . The prisoners shall be hanged by the neck, but not until they be dead, to be cut down alive, and their entrails to be taken out and burnt before their faces, and their heads cut off, and their bodies divided into four quarters, and their heads and quarters disposed of at the King's pleasure."

This declaration unmanned some of the accused, and they fell to weeping, some screaming out their innocence. The crowd erupted. We let rip with what we thought of those who had turned on the country that had given them shelter. I was loud, but Eric was louder still. His face was twisted and red with anger.

Soldiers mounted the wagons to secure the nooses to the braces. Once they were clear of the wagons, a shot was fired and the wagons were driven away, leaving the traitors to dangle at the ends of their ropes.

They did not die quickly. They writhed and kicked, their eyes bulging in their blood-engorged faces.

I screamed for blood with the best of the crowd, caught up in the wave of hatred flowing from them.

I joined in the chant of, "Quarter, quarter, quarter!" and booed and hissed when the bodies were taken down and only a symbolic cross — more of a scratch — was made on their torsos. The cheering reached a crescendo when the bodies were decapitated and the heads were fixed on pikes that were paraded in front of us, then stuck in the ground as a warning to all who harboured treasonous thoughts.

A group of men nearby were yelling, "Death to Yankees!" One among them cried out that all able-bodied men should march for the border and fight. His cry was taken up and I was the loudest. I knew that I had to do this.

Eric had been shouting all along, but now fell abruptly silent.

"Come, Eric!" I cried. "Let us be brothers in arms as well as brothers-in-law!" A blazing determination burned inside me. I *would* fight alongside Father and Angus and damn the consequences. The flush was fading from Eric's face and he struggled to meet my eyes. "I cannot," he said weakly. "Morag and the baby — there would be no one to help my father."

I could not hide my contempt. "Do what you see fit, but *I* am not a coward. I will go and do the duty that we both should owe. If you have not the stomach for it, you can help me, at least."

"Sandy, no! You should not be so rash. Don't get so carried away by the mood of the crowd. Your father is depending upon you."

Eric had paled and sweat beaded his forehead. He put a hand on my arm as if he would hold me back. I shook him off and moved away. Then I unbuckled the traces that harnessed Hamish to the wagon.

"Father will have no choice but to let me fight when I join him and Angus." My voice was steady and I hoped that Eric heard the determination it held. "Drew can manage as long as you take time out to oversee him and help him if he needs it." I stared hard at him.

He started to protest, but I cut him off, outlining the plan that was forming in my mind even as I spoke. "I will take Hamish. Go get me your saddle and harness your horse to the wagon, and take it back to my family. You can get a saddle from the barn and use it till I return. Tell my mother that I know she will worry, but that I cannot, as a son and brother, fail to stand alongside Father and Angus. Tell her it is what her brother would have done. Tell her that you will help Drew and that he can manage. It will not be long until we all return victorious!"

The fire of my own words sustained me as I

rode away, little caring what trouble I had caused behind me, or what lay ahead.

There were quite a few riding with me on the trail towards Niagara. Our spirits were high, but as the afternoon sun bore down, our numbers dwindled. Some just drifted away. Others made their excuses — feeble ones about cows to be milked or wives who would worry — and eventually there were just two left, myself and an old greybeard who must have been at least my grandfather's age. As we neared Stoney Creek, he slowed his horse and then stopped. Out of politeness, I pulled Hamish up alongside him. His expression was rueful and he shook his head as he spoke. "I am fooling no one but myself, boy," he said. "My fighting days are done. Even this ride has got every bone in my body aching. I'll not last a mile longer." He grinned at me, showing a few brownish-yellow stumps of teeth. "A fine boy like yourself, you'll make a difference. Go and give them what for. Strike a blow for me, too — Caleb Watson, who wishes he was in his prime once more!"

I couldn't help but smile as he shook his fist enthusiastically, only to wince as if it pained him, before turning his horse around and heading back the way we had come.

Hamish was not a young horse and as dusk

drew near, his pace slowed. I knew that soon I would have to stop. I was hungry, thirsty and tired because, in the fervour of the hangings, I had set off with no thought of food or drink. The landscape was familiar and I realised that I was close to Forty Mile Creek, where I had come to fetch Father and Angus from Van Camp's barn. From hearing Father talk, I knew there were two inns in the village and thought I would break my stay at whichever was cheapest.

On a whim, I turned Hamish and headed down the track that led to Van Camp's farm, curious to see whether Mathilda Van Camp remained and how she and her family were faring since her father had been declared traitor. I had not forgotten the kindness she had shown Father and Angus, kindness that had cost her dearly. Unlike my first visit, when the house had a sombre, closed-in feel, there was light in the windows and I could make out figures sitting on the veranda — men, by the loud voices and guffaws that rang out.

I dismounted and led Hamish towards them, calling out a greeting as I came. "Is this not the Van Camp farm?"

In answer I got no words, but one of the men leaped down and ran towards me. I caught a gleam of metal in his hand. "Who comes here, seeking that traitor?" he demanded. I saw that he held a knife.

My heart was beating fast. I had no weapon of my own. "No friend of his, sir," I stammered out. "Just Alexander MacKay of Ancaster on my way to join my father and brother, Robert and Angus MacKay, already at the border with the 5th Lincoln."

The fellow still regarded me suspiciously, tossing the knife from hand to hand. "What's your business with Van Camp, then?"

"None with him, but rather with his daughter, sir. She was kind to my father when he took sick and stayed here coming back from the battle at Queenston. I wanted to thank her and tell her that he was well again." I was cursing my impulsiveness and wishing I had stayed on the road.

The man spat at my feet. "Van Camp and his boys are riding with Willcocks and his damned Canadian Volunteers — although how *dare* they call themselves by that name. After what they did at Newark, none of those filthy Yankee-lovers will dare show their faces here again, not if they want to stay alive." He paused. "I've heard of the MacKays. Loyalists all, isn't that right, boy?"

I nodded, unsure of what he wanted me to say.

"We drove Van Camp's family off a while back."

He grinned. "Why shouldn't they suffer the same fate as the womenfolk of Newark, being thrown out of their homes with only what they stood up in."

I shivered, thinking of poor, cowed, kind Mathilda, and wondered where she might be with all turned against her because of her father. Lost in my thoughts, it took me a moment to realise that the fellow was still speaking to me.

"You're welcome to bed down here for the night, if you'd like." He no longer played with his knife and was smiling as he gestured towards the group on the veranda. "We've a roast piglet and beer."

I had not liked Van Camp, but the relish with which this man spoke of chasing away his defenceless womenfolk sat ill with me. I thanked him and made my excuses, saying that I had arranged to meet a family friend at one of the inns. I mounted Hamish and, as soon as I was out of sight, cajoled him into as fast a gallop as he could manage.

It was dark by the time I reached the inn and my side trip cost me any chance of a bed to myself, for the inn was full with people going to the border and also some who were fleeing north. Talk was wild, veering from how easily the Yankee army would be defeated, to how, after our loss at Chippawa, we should prepare ourselves for them to fight their way up and chase the British out of Burlington Heights. I listened as I ate my meal of boiled meat and pickled cabbage, but said nothing. It was obvious that all who could fight must try to prevent this invasion succeeding. And that included me.

I had to share a bed with a merchant from York who snored so badly that it was hard for me to sleep. I was up early the next morning, eager to eat and be on my way — so early, in fact, that I was the lone guest ready for breakfast. The innkeeper was sitting working on his accounts, but when he saw me he called out a name and a girl came out from the kitchen. I was stunned to see that it was Mathilda Van Camp. She kept her eyes lowered and did not look at me as she told me that she could prepare some eggs and bacon, and asked whether I would like beer or milk with my meal.

I reached out for her hand and spoke as gently as I could. Even so, she startled like a frightened rabbit and tried to wrench away. "Miss Van Camp, do not be afraid. I mean you no harm."

The use of her name seemed to scare her further and she pulled herself free, hunching herself over as if expecting a blow.

"You may not remember me," I said, "but you showed great kindness to my brother and father,

Robert and Angus MacKay, when they were in need." Still she would not look at me, so I continued, adding detail that might help her recall them and convince her that I meant no harm. "My father was sick and you persuaded your father to let them shelter in your barn. When I came to fetch them home, you gave me soup . . . "

She looked at me then, and I saw how thin she had become. "I remember you, sir, but times have changed," she said, her voice small and reedy. "It is not good to talk of my father here. It causes ill feeling and trouble I scarce need."

The innkeeper stirred himself and came over to us. "Is there something wrong, young man?"

"No, sir," I replied. "I recognised Miss Van Camp, who helped my father and brother some time ago, and was reminding her of that."

He grunted and I bristled, prepared to defend her if he treated her unkindly. "That's all right then," he said. "Mathilda suffers much because of what her father is, and I try to shield her when I can. That's why she cooks more than serves." He stalked off, leaving us alone once more.

"He has been very kind," Mathilda said. I could hear in those few words and her tone that many had not been.

"I went to your farm, before I came here," I said.

"I wanted to thank you and see how you were, as I heard your father was arraigned for treason. His name was read out at the Assizes."

Her face twisted bitterly. "No doubt you met the farm's new owners. I am sure they were happy to tell you what they had done."

I felt my face colour, as if by even listening to what had been done I was somehow party to it. I nodded.

"So, milk or beer?" Mathilda's tone was brisk, as if she wanted no more to be said.

"Beer," I muttered, thinking on how badly she had been treated and how the actions of one person could harm so many.

When Mathilda returned with my food, I asked her if she might sit so that I could tell her how her kindness most likely saved Father's life.

She sighed and after a quick nod to the innkeeper to indicate that all was well, sat at the bench opposite me.

I was hungry, so I am ashamed to say that I spoke between mouthfuls, but despite my lack of manners I gradually persuaded Mathilda to tell me what had befallen her.

"My father left us last summer, so yes, it is true that he was at Newark." She sighed and rested her head on her hands. "Who knows what he intended

— to come back and take us to America, or perhaps he thought the Americans would win and he could return in triumph. I cannot forgive him for what he left us to face."

"You said 'us' . . . so you are not entirely alone?" My words were meant to give hope, but tears rolled down her cheeks. She made no attempt to wipe them away.

When she spoke, I had to strain to hear her. "My two brothers rode with Father. It was just my mother and I left behind." It was almost as if Mathilda had forgotten about me, because the words that tumbled out had the feel of private thoughts, ones that she had had many times. "We knew there would be trouble when people realised where Father and the boys had gone, but we hoped it would not be more than nasty words. Newark changed that. When some of the survivors managed to struggle back, telling their stories, naming names, we knew it would be worse than words. No one would work on a traitor's farm. Mother and I tried so hard to keep the farm going just even a little. Then we'd hear men at night, riding round the farmhouse, trampling our vegetable garden, letting the chickens out from the coop for the foxes and coyotes to get. What could two women do against that?"

Mathilda looked at me and I hated her father and brothers for what they had done.

"When Father was declared a traitor at the Assizes, men came to our farm, claiming that all traitors' land was forfeit. Maybe it was. I don't know." She knuckled her eyes hard. "They told us to get out. When Mother tried to collect some clothes and goods, one of them lifted her up and threw her down the steps to the yard. We ran then, and John Ford — " She nodded in the direction of the innkeeper, who was still pretending to pore over his ledger. "He took us in, gave us shelter, although it has cost him dear in both reputation and income."

"Your mother works here, too?" I prompted, and was horrified when Mathilda started to sob and shake.

"Her mother died a week ago." The innkeeper spoke up and walked over, putting a grimy but gentle hand on Mathilda's shoulder. "She's got a home here with my wife and me, although it may take folks time to forget what her bastard father did."

"My mother would take her in," I blurted out without thinking, but once I'd said it I knew it was true. We had often talked of the girl who had defied her father to offer Angus and Father help.

"We live north of here in Ancaster. Maybe people there won't know the name Van Camp, or she could use another name." I was warming to this idea. Mathilda was about the same age as Polly and I knew that she and Mother would be happy to help Mathilda in her time of need, just as she had done for Father.

Mathilda was looking at me with tears still wet on her face, but with a tiny smile trembling on her lips. "She would?"

"Most definitely. If not for you, Father might have died."

The innkeeper and Mathilda looked at each other. He was the first to speak. "Will you take her there now?"

"I can't," I said, hating the way the hope on both their faces vanished so quickly. "I'm on my way to join the 5th Lincoln." I will admit that I said it in such a way as to imply that this was the normal course of events and not that I was a runaway. "But if you give me paper, I can write a letter to my mother that would tell her who Miss Van Camp is, and to offer her a safe haven."

"Would you, really?" Mathilda was holding her breath and did not release it until I nodded that I would.

A tiny smile quirked the corners of her mouth

when the innkeeper said he would take her to Mother.

Other people were starting to come down and Mathilda scurried back to the kitchen, leaving the innkeeper to serve their meals, while I hastily wrote the letter to Mother.

I did not set off as early as I had hoped, but when I did it was with hope in my heart that I had done some good, and that all further actions on this wild adventure would end as well. Hamish picked up on my mood and was almost spritely as we set off for Niagara.

It was a long day's riding, and more than once I saw British soldiers making steady progress south. Each time, I asked if they knew where I could find the 5th Lincoln, but only got vague answers that the militia were spread thin, guarding small settlements and dealing with American skirmishers who were set on causing as much mischief as they could.

I decided to head to Queenston, thinking I might find the Lincolns there, but the day was drawing to a close. I was hungry, too, not having eaten since leaving the Red Tavern, so it was not likely that I would make Queenston before darkness fell. I saw a track leading off the road and decided to take my chances and see if there was a farm at its end that would offer me a bed for the night. In the fading light I saw the outline of a house, but no candles flickered in the window. I tied Hamish to the rail of the porch and called out, "Hello, is anyone here?"

My voice sounded loud in the quiet of that clearing, but no reply came. I wondered where the owners of this farm were. Aware that it would soon be dark, I tried the handle of the door and went in. I could just make out the dim outlines of furniture, and saw cold ash in the hearth. On a table were cups and plates crusted with congealed food. Whoever lived here must have left in a hurry.

I felt ill at ease being uninvited, but my growling stomach reminded me that I needed to eat. I found a muslin-wrapped wheel of cheese in a chest to the side of the table. A chunk of that and water I drew from the well stopped the hunger pangs. I could not bring myself to further intrude, so rather than take a cot in the house, I chose to bed down for the night in the outbuilding to one side where there were two boxes for horses. Hamish had one and I the other, and I have to say that he made less noise than Angus, so I slept well. I must have been more tired than I realised, because the sun was high in the sky by the time I woke.

I think that I would have slept even longer had I not heard a bellowing and mooing outside fit to raise the devil. It was obvious that the cow making the noise had not been milked in some time. She had probably been turned loose when her owners fled. I found a leather bucket and quickly milked her. Then I decided to waste no more time, so I fed and watered Hamish and mounted him, ready to set off once again for Queenston.

I heard hoof beats coming down the track from the road, so fast that I had no time to do anything before a group of men burst into the clearing. My heart started to race when I saw that they wore grey jackets, just like the Americans wore. About twenty men on horseback, all armed, blocked the entrance to the track.

One spoke up, leering at me and riding close enough to cause Hamish to sidestep uneasily. "What have we here, boys? A spy? A stray militia-man? Or just a farmer's boy about to run away?"

I hesitated, unsure of what to say. The Americans laughed at me, perhaps mistaking my silence for fear. I had to think fast, to try to wheedle my way out of this situation. I could not tell the truth — not unless I wanted my military career to be over before it even started. "I am from Ancaster, sir. It's on the road to York."

The man who had spoken first did not allow me to continue. "You're a long way from home then and you have me wondering why. I see no weapons."

"My grandfather, sir — a smith — lives near the Falls. I have instructions to bring him to Ancaster, away from the fighting that is sure to occur here." I tried to sound as if I were scared, when really I wanted to scream defiance at these invaders. "He is old and alone and has no family but us."

"A smith, you say?" The man scratched his chin thoughtfully. "John Thornton," he suddenly bellowed, causing Hamish to skitter even more. "Your horse is about to throw a shoe, is it not? You've been whining and holding us back for the last hour. I think we have a solution to your trials." He grinned wolfishly at me.

I cursed myself for embroidering my speech with details, which really should not have been said. The last thing I wanted was to lead our enemy to my grandfather's smithy.

"Get down off your horse, boy!"

I stared at him and did not move.

He drew a pistol from his belt and cocked it, pointed it at me and repeated his instruction. His eyes gleamed and I knew that he would not hesitate to shoot, so I scrambled down off Hamish's back and stood beside him.

"Unsaddle him!"

I wasted no time and did as I was told. When he gave Thornton a similar order, I saw what was to happen. They were taking Hamish and leaving me with a horse going lame. I felt a lump in my throat, and as I worked I patted Hamish and spoke soothingly to him, hating what now lay ahead of him. It was a poor reward for a horse that had given us such faithful service.

My fingers were clumsy. Thornton had his horse unsaddled and was standing impatiently by as I fumbled with the buckles on the cinch. As soon as I had pulled the saddle off, he set to work immediately. I moved towards his horse with my saddle, but the one in charge stepped in front of me, blocking my way.

"Not so fast, boy!" he said. He was smiling still, but his eyes never left my face. "We can't have you running off to raise the alarm that we are in the area, can we?"

"I won't tell. I promise!" I would have said anything to make them leave me alone.

The man laughed. "That promise would last until we rode off. No, I am not going to take any chances. Even if Thornton's limping nag would leave you on foot, a strapping boy like you could be in the nearest village with a couple of hours' walking." His men snickered and hooted at that, though I did not see any humour in it. "I think we should detain you a little."

Before I could protest further, he signalled two of his men. They grabbed my arms. I bucked and tried to wrench myself free, but their grip was strong. In desperation, I let myself go limp, giving them dead weight to drag. All this did was earn me a blow that made my teeth clack together and my senses spin. When my awareness returned, four of them were half lifting, half dragging me towards the outbuilding. Another was waiting in the doorway holding rope.

"No," I screamed, and tried once more to free myself.

The Americans' leader strode over and thrust his pistol to my head, cocking it again. "One more sound from you and I will splatter your brains to kingdom come." His tone was low but menacing. I was certain he would not hesitate to shoot.

It took them but a minute to hog-tie me and dump me onto the floor of the outbuilding. I was thankful that they did not close the door and leave me in darkness, for I doubt I could have borne that.

I don't know how long I lay there, cursing my predicament, but it seemed hours that I was forced to listen to the raucous shouting of the Americans, the anguished bellowing of the cow, shots being fired, and the sounds of wood being broken and china smashing. I struggled against my bonds, but I had been tied up by men who knew what they were doing. All I did was make the ropes tighten and cut painfully into my wrists and ankles. I am ashamed to say that I cried — angry tears because nothing was going right for me. Those tears eventually brought sleep.

* * *

All was silent when I woke. The weak, early morning sun was rising above mist. I ached all over from my night on the hard, wooden floor. My wrists and ankles felt raw from my struggles and my bladder was painfully full. Tears threatened again as I realised the hopelessness of my position. Unless someone came, I could die here. I roared out as loud as I could, calling for help, but knew it was a foolish thing to do. I tried to wriggle my way out of the doorway and was making good if painful progress when suddenly I could move no more. Something held me fast. The bastards had tied my ropes to something I couldn't see.

Neighing startled me out of my morass of self-pity, but I decided it was only the lame horse left in exchange for Hamish. Hope only came when I realised that I could hear the sound of a horse's hooves, hooves that seemed to be moving at a steady pace. I hollered for all I was worth and kept going, hardly stopping for breath until I heard the jingle of stirrups and bridle.

A voice called out, "Who's there? Show yourself!"

"In the outbuilding. I'm tied up. Yankee scouts, damn their eyes, surprised me yesterday." I winced as I realised that I had no guarantee that this man was not an American, too.

The sun was suddenly blocked out as a figure loomed over me. He was dressed, to my relief, in ordinary working clothes.

He crouched down and, with quick fingers, untied me and helped me to stand. I groaned as pins and needles prickled my hands and feet. My head was ringing and pounding and it was several minutes until I could speak or look my rescuer over.

"Take your time, lad." His voice was kindly and he patted me on the shoulder. "Then you can tell me what happened here." He gestured with his free hand. I looked up to find a scene of devastation. The neat gardens in the yard had been trampled. Scattered among the broken plants were smashed pots, furniture, even clothes that had obviously been dragged from the house. In the middle of this senseless destruction lay the poor cow, her sides hacked and carved where they had taken meat from her. I hung my head, not wanting to look at what could so easily be our own snug farm, if the Yankees won.

"Bastards!" I spat out.

The man said, "I share your sentiments, son, but not your choice of words." He shook his head in sorrow and disbelief. "Years of labour gone. And poor Clover, too. My children will cry when I tell them. I knew there were American scouts nosing around, so I thought it would be safer if I took my family to St. Davids to shelter with my brother there." He cleared his throat and continued. "What a mistake! The Yankees came and chased the 1st Lincoln out. After that they did what they liked, taking what they pleased, then burning the houses. We were helpless. My brother lost everything." His eyes were wet with tears as he struggled to contain his emotions. "We stood by and watched them as they laughed and shouted, making mock of us. Once they left, I waited a while, not wanting to run into them again, then came to see whether it was safe to return." He gestured at the destruction. "And I find this."

"At least they did not burn your home here," I offered. It was poor comfort, but true.

"You're right, boy. I will bring my family and my brother's family, too, and we'll get it shipshape again." He paused. "But how did you come to be here?"

My whole sad story poured out. When I told him of my intention to seek out the 5th Lincoln in Queenston, he shook his head again and snorted. "Think again. The Americans have taken Queenston, too. You'd do best to head back towards Twelve Mile Creek, as I think that's where they might be, under Major General Riall. Or even head to the Falls or Fort George in Newark."

My heart sank. How would I find them? "I'll head for the Falls, sir, where my grandfather, John Livesay, has a smithy. Perhaps he will have news of the Lincolns."

"I know your grandfather — a good man. I wish I could help you get there, but I must tend to my own family. Tell him that you met Isaac Bowman and what happened here. You have a long walk ahead of you, so take care. If you can find food in this mess, you are welcome to it."

As he remounted, turning to ride off, I ran quickly to the side of the house to deal with my bursting bladder. As I relieved myself, thoughts churned in my head. I had lost Hamish. Eric's saddle at least was still in the yard where I had dropped it, but it would be heavy and awkward to carry. Father was going to be furious. It occurred to me that although the Americans had killed the farmer's beast, there was no sign of Thornton's horse. I doubted that they would take it, for their leader had been complaining of how it hampered them. I decided to search the woods for the horse — it could bear Eric's saddle, at least. My first task, however, was to try to fill my empty belly.

As I approached the house, I heard a soft whicker and found the horse cropping grass under an apple tree. I backed away quietly, in case I spooked it, and got the saddle, bag and tackle from the front yard where the Americans had left it. I thanked God that I had kept my moneybag in my breeches and they had not searched me, for it was obvious that they had rifled through the saddlebag. The horse hardly stopped eating when I threw the halter over its head. It resisted just a little when I led it round the house and tied it to the porch rail while I gathered the meagre amounts of food left unspoiled.

The afternoon sun was hot as we walked. The horse favoured one leg and I swear he walked slower than even Sam would have done. I was sweating and sore. Relief only came when dusk fell. I knew that there was still some way to go and that it would be foolish to continue in the dark. I had seen few people on the road. Perhaps most were staying quiet because of Yankee patrols. No dwellings were in sight and, to tell the truth, I was now wary of being caught like before, so I led the horse — I had decided to call it Madison, after the Yankee president — into a copse of trees where we could spend the night in relative safety. There was a small stream, so at least we had water.

I did not rest easy. Every noise startled me from sleep. Several times I heard shouting in the distance, even musket fire. As dawn broke I set off once again. Even at that early hour, the road was busy. Troops from both sides were everywhere, scouting, to try to work out where the other had its main force. Still, the bustle could not drown out the roar of the Falls.

I must have looked such a forlorn sight that any soldiers who saw me decided I was no danger, nor likely to be of any use to them, for I was left alone.

From one British patrol I did glean that the 5th Lincoln had indeed been at Twelve Mile Creek, but were likely on the move by now. A farmer with a cart confirmed that John Livesay's forge was just half a mile away on the Portage Road, and after this welcome news it seemed just a few minutes until I stumbled in through the wide doors of my grandfather's smithy.

He had his back to me, working the bellows furiously, and didn't hear me at first. When he did turn, expressions of surprise, curiosity and even a hint of anger slid across his face.

"Alexander, what in heaven's name are you doing here and in such a bedraggled state?" He frowned, a look of worry replacing all other emotions. "Is it bad news you bring, of your mother, or of your father and Angus?" His hand shook as it held onto one of the bellows' handles.

"No, no," I hurried to reassure him. "I've come to join Father and Angus with the Lincolns, to fight alongside them."

"And this is with your mother's knowledge?" he asked.

I was glad that he had phrased his question the way he had, for I could honestly answer it. "Aye, sir, she knows where I am and what I am doing. Eric Holzer, Morag's husband, will be helping Drew until we all return in triumph!" I congratulated myself on speaking nothing but truth, allowing him to assume what he would from the little I told him.

Grandfather smiled at that. "We all hope that will be the case. But Sandy, look at the state of you

— as if you have been dragged through a hedge backwards. And you stink. You've had a hard journey, it would seem."

His kind words acted like a key. Once the door was open, all that had happened with the Yankee patrol poured out of me. I could see that he had questions, but he held them back until I finished, and it was the measure of the man that he attended to the practicalities first.

"Sandy, where is this American horse? I should at least see to the poor beast. While I do that, clean yourself and then we'll talk." He laughed and said, "I have no clothes that will fit a young giant, but take a nightshirt from my chest and wash your clothes, too. In this hot weather, they'll dry soon."

Having taken Grandfather to Madison, I ducked my head through the low front door of the cottage and went inside. Mother often fretted that since my grandmother's death, Grandfather must be struggling to take care of himself, but the neatness of the room gave no evidence of that. The floor was swept clean and the room tidy. A meal was cooking in a pot hanging over the fire.

I was so hot that bathing in a cool creek seemed like an idea made in heaven itself. I had my shirt and britches off in seconds and threw myself into the water, happy to wash off the dust of the road and to wallow in the water like a hog in mud. There were, however, things that could not be washed away — cuts and bruises from my tussle with the Yankees. I boiled inside, thinking of their arrogance.

I probably did a poor job with my clothes, but I was too tired to care. Grandfather's nightshirt fit in the shoulders, for years at his forge had made him brawny, but it was far too short. I must have looked a ridiculous sight with it ending just above my knees. By the time I re-entered the cottage, he was sitting at the table waiting for me. He handed me a tankard of ale. "Food, then sleep are what you need, my boy," Grandfather said. "I doubt that we will see either your father or brother tonight, for they called here yesterday when they were out on patrol, but tomorrow you can try to catch up with them. I'm sure that if we ask in the village, someone will be able to direct you to them."

"They were *here?*" I said. "I just missed them?"

Grandfather didn't answer right away. He rose and ladled out two bowls from the pot hanging on the fire, and fetched a warm loaf out from the oven. I swear that food has never tasted so good, either before or since. It was rabbit, and there were potatoes and carrots. Grandfather did not speak or let me speak until he had given me my second bowl and I had slowed down a little.

I tried again. "Father and Angus were well?" I asked.

"Yes," Grandfather said. "They call in when they can, but the militia have been kept busy dealing with American patrols. Your encounter attests to the fact that the blackguards are out scouting, looking for weakness. Some say that they will push towards Burlington Heights, but I am sure our fellows will do their very best to thwart such a plan."

He paused and used a knob of the bread to wipe his bowl clean, popping it into his mouth, chewing and swallowing it before speaking again. "Poor Hamish, he was a good horse." He sighed. "Let's hope that he comes to no harm. The horse you got is a good one, too, now that I have reshod him — young, but strong and placid. Your father will only be a little put out by such an exchange, but . . . " He looked amused. "I'll warrant that he will give you grief about the loss of a musket and shot."

I nearly blurted out, "What musket?" but managed to stop myself in time, for Grandfather's words neatly presented me with a solution to a problem that I had not even realised I had, until he spoke — my lack of a weapon. I tried to look as hangdog as I could. "That he will, sir, and I must hope that there will be a spare when I join them."

The words I was angling for came from his lips without hesitation. "Take mine, Sandy, and make good use of it. I wish I could be there alongside Rob, Angus and you, but you will be a fine substitute. But," he added, "only if you get some sleep, for I have never seen eyes that struggle so much to stay open."

He was right. It was all I could do to stumble up the ladder to the sleeping loft and fall upon the straw tick.

When I woke up, the sun was once again high in the sky, burning down. In my surprise, I cracked my head hard on a beam as I reared up. My clothes, neatly folded, lay by the side of the tick. I dressed hurriedly and slid down the ladder, only to find the cottage empty. Two horses were tethered to the rail outside the forge and when I went in, Grandfather was in conversation with two British officers. Their conversation broke off at my entry and Grandfather waved me forward. "This is my grandson, come to join his father and brother with the militia, the one I told you about — a fine addition, is he not? He's looking for the 5th Lincoln. Would you know where he might find them?"

I blushed a little at my grandfather's obvious pride, but perked up when one of the officers said, "There are rumours that an American army, some five thousand strong, have left Chippawa and are marching to the Falls, to camp here before moving on. When that report reaches Major General Riall, I'm sure he will send part of his force forward to block them. Most likely the 5th Lincoln will be included."

Grandfather shook his head and sucked air in between his clenched teeth. "A bad business. Let's hope they get no farther than the Falls."

I burned with impatience to set off as Grandfather continued his conversation. When the officers finally left, I asked Grandfather for his musket and shot. He sighed, but gave them to me, telling me that Father and Angus were probably only a mile away. "Stay safe, Sandy, and listen to your father," were the last words he said as he hugged me hard.

When I drew close to the junction at Portage Road I saw a fine array of British troops and militia spread out across a small hill, in the fields and even in the woods. I began to wonder what greeting I would get from Father, and how to prevent him from sending me back to Grandfather — or more likely home like a whipped puppy.

I was heartened to see so many already there,

and to be told by a sentry that reinforcements from both Twelve Mile Creek, led by Riall himself, and from York were expected. I was convinced that although we might be smaller in number, we would soon send any Americans packing, and received a clap on the back for saying so. Apart from the sentries, many of the men were taking their ease. Some were even trying to sleep, for they had marched through the night. I briefly considered staying where I was and attaching myself to another Lincoln unit, but honour would not let me take such an easy route. My intention was to stand alongside my brother and father to protect our land, and I would have to face Father's anger first in order to do that. The 5th Lincoln were on the right flank, so I worked my way across the hilltop until I spotted their commander, Colonel Bradt, ride up and dismount.

As I picked my way between men, carefully stepping over sleeping bodies, Angus spotted me first. He leaped to his feet, dropped the musket he had been cleaning, and stared at me, mouth open, as if he were catching flies.

"Where's Father?" I asked before he could speak.

"He and the other sergeants are with the officers. The main American force is at Chippawa, but we expect them to move forward." Angus shook his head. "You're doing what you always do, Sandy, befuddling me with a question. What in tarnation are *you* doing here?"

There was no point now in being anything but honest. I told Angus straight what I had done and why. He did not interrupt, but I gauged his reactions by the expressions that flickered across his face: horror at my description of the hangings; sadness to hear of Mathilda Van Camp's plight; amused irritation when I said that no matter what, I was staying. I finished by saying that I would hide from Father's sight if need be, but that I was going to fight and nothing would stop me.

"Ah, Sandy, you're so headstrong!" Angus's tone was half admiring. "I don't know where you find the strength to challenge things as you do. Come here." He gave me a fierce hug. "I will be proud to have you fight alongside me, but now we have to convince Father to let you stay, and that might not be easy."

I could not settle. I kept one eye out for Father's return at all times, and in the end Angus checked my musket for me rather than see me fumble with it. He shared some rations he had in his pack and suggested that I try to sleep, as he was going to do. From where we sat in the shade of a tree, I could see Father in a huddle of men — he was easy to recognise, as he stood so much taller than the others. The Hatt brothers were there too, along with Colonel Bradt and John Lee. When the conclave ended, Mr. Lee and Father walked back together, deep in conversation.

It was Mr. Lee who spotted me as I leapt nervously to my feet. "MacKay, you have both your boys here now!" he said, clapping Father on the back. "You did not say that young Sandy was coming. It's a good thing, too, if the scouts are to be believed and the American army is moving our way in such force." He was oblivious to the way Father was reacting, his face first blanching and then setting in anger as he stared at me. "I'll go find my rascal Jack and tell him that his companion in arms is back." He set off, grinning. I wished that Father were so happy to see me.

Angus had been awakened by Mr. Lee's loud voice and stood behind me, one hand on my shoulder. I was grateful for that touch. It gave me courage to speak. "Father, I know you didn't want me to be part of this, but after what I saw at Burlington Heights, the hangings . . . " I shuddered as the image of those twisted, purpling faces rose unbidden in my mind. "And the rumours I heard of the Americans being about to attack, I just had to come." I thought that if I kept talking I could stave off his anger, so I hurried on. "What good am I working on the farm if the Americans break through here and move towards Burlington Heights and even our own home? Mother knows where I am. She will not be happy, but then if the Americans win . . . " I did not voice what horror that would bring her. "Eric Holzer is helping Drew and Polly to keep the farm going; he promised me that. They can manage. And if we have victory here and rout our enemies once and for all, we can all be home in a matter of days."

Father tried to break in, but I kept going, adding details that I thought would help my case. "I spent a night at Grandfather's and he has wished me well. He even gave me his own musket and shot, saying that I fight in his stead."

Father surprised me. As I spoke, the anger faded from his face and his shoulders drooped. "Oh, you foolish, foolish boy," he said as he stepped forward to embrace me. Then he pushed me back and, holding me at arm's length, said, "If I shut my eyes and just listen, it could be your Uncle Roger talking to your mother's father, trying to convince him he was old enough to fight." He looked upward. "Is it always going to be the province of the young to be so foolhardy and brave?"

I could see tears glistening in the corners of his eyes. "I'll make you proud, Father, I promise," I said.

"I know you think that, Sandy." Father's voice was gentle. "And you do and will. But now I have to worry about both Angus and you." He tried to laugh, but the sound died in his throat. "Your mother will skin me alive if I let anything happen to her boys. All those arguments you have given me — about how your size and strength will be an asset, that I have trained you to be as good a shot as any — they are all true. But while they will be a help, luck is what you need most in a battle. I pray that we will all have that in the next few hours."

Angus, who had been silent till now, stepped alongside me. "Are we to fight then? Is that what you were told?" I heard no eagerness in his voice. No fear either, just resignation. An excited anticipation surged up inside me.

"Aye, by the end of the day for sure," Father said. He let his hands drop from my shoulders to his sides. "The American army is on the move from Chippawa and heading this way. We have to stop them here. Let's rest our bones while we can." He sat down. "But for the Yankees pushing north, I would send you back to your Grandfather, Sandy, but I daren't risk it now."

He rested his hands on his knees, straightened his back, then said, "My duties may take me away once the fighting starts, but I want you both to promise me that you will stick together and look out for each other." The urgency in his voice had us both swearing that we would, our voices overloud as we tried to prove our sincerity. This seemed to ease his mind, for he stretched himself out in the shade, and said, "Rest now, while you can. It is likely to be a long and hard night."

I knew I would not sleep, but I lay down, as did Angus. We shared his pack as a hard and knobby pillow. None of us spoke, and for the first time, a little fear rose inside me and lodged in my chest like a stone. I glanced first at Angus, who lay on his back, his breathing regular, and his eyes closed, and then at Father, who was staring back at me, his eyes wide in his pale face. I could not stand that steady stare, so closed my eyes, trying not to think about what was coming.

I doubt that any slept as afternoon faded to evening. The constant roar of the Falls, shouts as scouts returned, even an occasional crack of a musket, all combined to keep sleep at bay. By about six, word came that Americans had been seen nearby and in considerable force, as close as Willson's Tavern down by Table Rock, and all became confusion as the order to retreat to Queenston was given. I was aghast. I had come to fight, and now was being ordered to flee like a whipped cur without even trying to repel the American force. Many men were grumbling and being deliberately slow to move, until Father and the other sergeants hurried them along.

I did not understand the thinking behind that order or why it was quickly countermanded. Some said that Lieutenant General Drummond, fresh that day from York, had stopped the retreat, loudly berating Major General Riall for a coward, his face as scarlet as his uniform. We had only gone a mile before we were ordered to turn smartly around and form our battle line along the ridge of Lundy's Lane, around the church on the hilltop. Our guns, four in all, plus a rocket division and a howitzer, were planted in the cemetery on a gentle slope. The blue-coated artillerymen struggled to get everything in place quickly, the guns' muzzles facing towards the open space in front of the chestnut woods. The British regulars formed up behind the guns on the hill. On the left flank, curving gently down the slope by the Portage Road, were more redcoats and some of our incorporated militia. The 5th Lincoln were at the far edge of the right flank of the battle line, alongside the Glengarry Light Infantry and Captain John Norton's warriors. I had met John Norton when he visited our village, and a handsome man he was, but now he and his warriors were fearsome sights with their topknots and grim, painted faces. I was glad they were not my enemies. Some stayed in the battle line while others drifted like smoke into the woods.

There was a stillness like none I had ever experienced before. It was as if time had stopped, or rather that I had stepped outside it. Every sense was heightened.

I heard birds singing, the ragged sound of Angus's breath as he stood alongside me, my own heart — which seemed so loud that it must shake my body — the rushing waters of the great cataract. Not a man in the ranks spoke. Raw and untrained though I was, I knew from Father and Angus that I should not speak either, just concentrate on hearing the orders the sergeants would relay to us.

Shadows were creeping down the hill where we waited. I could not see anything but the broad back of George Markle in front of me. I wondered whether Markle hoped to bring glory to his family name and erase the shame of his traitorous relative, Abraham. From the way Markle's spine stiffened, I knew that the American soldiers were in sight, coming out of the trees and forming up on the flat, open meadow below the hill. They would be waiting for the order to fire, just as we were. I wanted to close my eyes, but dared not. For long minutes I saw nothing more than the worn threads of a jacket, the grime embedded in a sunburned neck, a queue of brown hair that was slowly losing a battle to grey.

It was hot, even though the day was drawing to a close, so hot that we all were sweating. I had drunk from my canteen just a little time ago, but my mouth was parched and dry, as though it would never be anything else ever again. There was an odd taste there, metallic, but rotten, too — the taste of fear.

The world exploded. The hill shook to its roots as our cannons opened up, a deep rumble that travelled through my body, leaving me feeling hollowed out. My ears rang with the booming of the guns and my eyes smarted from the bitterness of the smoke that blew all around us. In that cacophony, I could still make out the familiar sound of my father's deep voice. "Prepare! Aim! Fire!"

George did just that, then dropped to one knee so that I might do so, too. All those times I had secretly practised loading Father's musket in the barn stood me in good stead — my fingers did not fumble too much, but I was slow, tamping down the powder, inserting the shot and cocking the trigger. I had barely got my shot off, and I can't say that I aimed at all, before George was rising, ready to shoot again. We kept at it — loading, firing, and not thinking, not able to see whether our shots were true. Time had no meaning for me. It could have been five minutes or fifty minutes. The British guns pounded away and so much smoke rose up that it was hard to see what was happening ahead of us. The Americans were being beaten bloody, but they held firm and kept firing, although they were too far away for their musket balls to reach us. After our first few rounds we were given the order to cease fire and stood there silent, watching the slaughter take place below us, wondering why the American commander did not give the order to retreat, as the Yankees were so badly outgunned.

As smoke cleared briefly, Angus gripped my arm and pointed. I gaped at what I saw. The Americans, despite the pounding they were taking, were trying to advance towards the British guns, bringing them into even closer range. Raised voices shouted orders, and suddenly the Glengarries, who had stood at our side, were on the move, marching forward to form a skirmish line in the trees alongside a farm track, a move that would put them in position to attack the American flank.

My mouth went dry again as I waited to hear whether we would be given the order to move forward. I checked my musket, gripping it as tightly as I could. The light was fading, but musket flashes showed where the enemy position lay. My heart skipped a beat when word came that we were to move forward in support.

I thought that our lines would march proudly forward, and then stop and fire, but this was a different kind of warfare. A ragged collection of Lincolns, the 2nd Yorks and Norton's warriors advanced, hugging every bit of cover we could find — broken-down fences, trees, shrubs, even gravestones for those on the left who were nearer to the guns.

The Yorks' commanding officer did not accompany them, choosing to hide behind a shed. Some of our own men slipped away into the growing darkness at the top of the hill rather than start on down it. I cursed them for cowards and was proud that I did not hesitate, but silently followed Angus and Father into the fray.

We fired at will, but it was impossible to see what effect our muskets had. The Americans fired back, but sporadically. Were their losses now so great that few remained, or was their ammunition low? Angus and I were crouched behind a shrub, rising to shoot in turn. Father and George Markle were placed a little to our left. I was waiting my turn to fire when a shout of pain erupted from my left. My world stood still, for I could not tell who had cried out — Father or George. I was frozen in place and would have stayed like that had not Angus pulled me into motion, whispering hoarsely, "Come, Sandy, George is shot." I had not realised I was holding my breath until Angus's words released me.

We edged our way to Father and George's position, grateful for the shelter of darkness. Father was down, too, and an icy splinter of fear pierced my heart until I realised that George had fallen on him and he was struggling to free himself.

"Boys, come quick," he hissed as he managed to crouch down by George. "He's taken a musket ball to the chest, I think. We need to get him to safety."

It was impossible to see the extent of George's wound, but he was white-faced and shaking, his eyes fixed on something that we could not see. His entire right side was wet with blood — blood that showed black in the dim light.

"George. George!" Father gripped his left shoulder. "Can you hear me? We'll get you to safety, but it would help if you can walk."

George gave no answer but a groan, sounding more like an animal than a man.

Father rocked back on his heels and ran a hand down his face. "We cannot leave him here. We'll have to carry him back up the hill."

I flinched at the thought, as George, although not tall, was a solidly built man.

Father gathered George's musket, then reached out his free hand for our muskets, too. "You two are stronger than I am. Angus, take his shoulders. Sandy, take his feet, and go as fast as you can. I will be close behind."

The MacKay boys' strength was never more needed. We flew up the slope, crouched over like dogs, pursued by the whizzing wasps of musket balls, not stopping until we were safely behind our own lines. I feared that our frantic run had killed poor George, as his head was hanging loosely and bobbing between his shoulders, but he groaned when we laid him down.

Other wounded were trickling back, some walking, others carried — and we were told to move George to the farmhouse just a little to the side of our original position. The lady of the house, pale-faced and weeping, told us to set him on her kitchen floor. This we did, horrified to see how many wounded already lay there.

When we emerged from the farmhouse the guns had all fallen silent, but along with the roar of the Falls, I could hear voices giving orders — on both sides, I presumed — and the sounds of men moving in the dark. Worst of all were the screams and moans from the injured that lay in the dark, terrified they might be abandoned. I was eager to take up the fight once more, but my hopes were cruelly dashed. Colonel Bradt was striding along with a pair of redcoats by his side, both of them carrying sacks. When he came to us he said, "MacKay, hand over your ammunition and that of your boys. It's going to the regulars! Accompany these soldiers to get the ammunition from the rest of our men."

"Sir, we can *fight*, you know that!" Father shot back.

Colonel Bradt's face darkened and he bellowed, "Damn you, MacKay, are you questioning my orders? I was nearly killed by the wild shooting of my *own* men. Do as you're told and report back to me for further orders. Leave the shooting to those who know what they are doing!"

Father was furious, but he held back the words I guessed he wanted to say and with a quiet, "Sir!"

turned on his heel and marched stiffly off, the two redcoats trailing behind him like a pair of lost puppies.

Angus and I set off after Father, but had only gone a few steps when the colonel bellowed, "You two don't need to help your father. Bring back more wounded. Ours first. Only bring theirs if you can find none of ours. At least we can show the damned British that we have *some* uses." He stalked off, muttering angrily under his breath.

Before we set off to find our wounded, a cheer went up from our fellow soldiers — reinforcements from Twelve Mile Creek had arrived. Even though I smarted that I would not be in the actual fighting, at least our victory was assured. I could not stop my face splitting in a grin.

I turned to Angus and, as calmly as if I were asking him to take a walk with me, said, "Shall we?" I pointed down the hill to where our guns were bombarding the enemy. I suspected that we would find many wounded artillerymen in need of rescue, since their positions had been closest to the Yankees.

We started to run down the hill, aware that other militiamen were moving down, too, some carrying ammunition, others empty-handed and probably charged with the same task as us.

We arrived in the midst of the guns as they started up again, but this time they were not firing at an American force frozen in place like sitting ducks. Now they were under attack.

It was hell. I have no other word for it, even though I know Mother would blanch to hear me say it. Thunderous noise, fire from the mouths of our cannons, the shuddering recoil of those guns, musket balls whizzing through the air, the screaming of the injured and dying on both sides, smoke filling my lungs, the stench of blood and shit — all of these assaulted my senses.

I was hacking and spluttering. Angus was faring no better. A sergeant yelled to us, pointing to a man on the ground by his side. What the man's wound was I never found out. We were struggling to lift him, and even for us it was a struggle — gunners have to be fine, strapping men — when the Americans broke through and were amongst us.

Bayonets flashed in the moonlight, and sabres, too, as the officers cut and slashed for all they were worth. Some of the gunners snatched up muskets and fired blindly at our attackers. Angus and I were weaponless — in danger not only from the enemy but also from the wild shooting of our own men. I snatched a ramrod lying beside one of the cannons and called to Angus to stay close.

I jabbed and poked at any Americans who came near. One tall fellow dropped his musket, grabbed the ramrod and tried to pull it from my hands. I clung on, desperate not to lose the only protection we had. He swore as he tried to yank it from me. Angus stepped from behind me and, with all his strength, hit the man in the face. Blood gushed instantly. He cried out and brought his hands up to his shattered nose. With the ramrod free, I swung it hard, catching him on the side of the head. He dropped like a poleaxed cow. Angus quickly grabbed the man's musket from the ground. We stood back to back, ready for any attackers — me with the ramrod and Angus with the bayonet.

The order to retreat came and we ran.

The fighting was thick around us, but many were now trying to flee to the safety of our own lines. It made us easy targets and the Yankees were quick to take advantage, firing at our retreating backs. With musket balls flying by, I felt a surge of fear that it would end here. I ran in a blind panic.

Angus must have had similar thoughts. "Head for the trees close to the left flank!" he cried.

His words made sense. If we could reach the woods, then it would be easier to evade the Americans and work our way back up the slope and across to find Father and the rest of the Lincolns.

I ran like I've never run before — head down, fists pushing against the air as if I could tear my way through it, my lungs burning from the smoke that swathed the battlefield. I ran over bodies in my path, leaping over them if I could, trampling them when I could not. Finally I crashed through underbrush and into the woods. In my panic I flung myself headfirst beneath a tree, unable to speak until my breathing slowed and my voice returned. I dared not shout, lest our enemies were hiding here, too, so I whispered as loud as I could, "Angus, Angus, where are you?"

No answer came, so I cautiously sat up and peered around. I tried again, as loud as I dared. "Angus, call out and let me know you are safe."

I heard it then, a faint call a little farther up the slope, in the trees. I crawled on my belly in the direction of the call and soon saw the outline of a figure propped up against a tree.

"Angus!"

It was only when I went to embrace him that I realised that this man was too small and slight to be my brother.

"I'm not Angus, but will an Abell do?" The voice was quiet, perhaps even a little weak. There was a hint of amusement as he carried on. "They both start with *A* and have the same number of letters."

It was so dark under the tree that I could not see what uniform the speaker wore, just the pale glimmer of his face. "Who are you, sir?" he continued. "Don't be afeared. I offer no threat to you."

He was young, judging by his voice — the voice of a boy who had not yet reached manhood. He tried to laugh, but seemed to choke a little before he sputtered out, "Do you mean me harm?"

I sank back on my heels, then lowered myself to sit by him. "No, I don't," I said. I could not fight down the sob that ripped its way up from deep within my chest. "My brother Angus and I were at the cannons and he was behind me, and we were running. He was right on my heels. He told me to make for the trees. Now I can't find him. I *have* to find him." I dashed tears from my eyes and tried to get to my feet, but the boy grasped my sleeve and held on.

"No, stay. It would be madness to go out from here." His voice was low, the tone urgent. "In the dark you'll not find him, only get yourself killed in the process. Look out there, and tell me that I don't speak true." He sighed. "I got separated, too, but they'll come looking for me when they can. Sergeant Dunkley promised my mother he'd keep me close. Your brother will come looking for you, too, I'm sure."

I tried to do as he said and peered out from the woods. All I could see was smoke, dim forms struggling within it, a writhing, shapeless mass. It would be hopeless trying to find Angus in that. I just prayed that he had found a place to take shelter.

"Sir, you know my name, Abell, but you haven't given me yours."

"Sandy MacKay." I didn't want to sit making idle conversation, and decided that I would wait until there was a lull in the fighting and try to go up the slope.

"Well, Sandy MacKay, Abell Phillips of Pennsylvania is glad for your company. I was scared here all by myself. I keep hearing movement in the trees. Voices, too, and I didn't know what manner of men they might belong to."

"Pennsylvania!" In my shock, my voice came out louder than was wise. I froze, thinking it might draw attention to our hiding place. "You're American." I kept my voice low but I knew it betrayed my feelings. Abell still had hold of my arm and I tried to shake myself free, but he held on with surprising tenacity.

"And you are not," he said. He sounded tired. "I thought that likely, as you wear no uniform. Me, I'm no soldier, just a drummer boy who joined

Porter's Brigade for a lark and to see a little more of the world than our farm near Mansfield." Still keeping his grip on my arm, he shifted slightly, as if uncomfortable. The small movement caused him to groan.

"Are you hurt?"

"I don't know. Perhaps I am. But just a little." He tried to move again. "Something hit me and knocked me down, and when my senses returned, here I was. Someone might have carried me — I have no recollection of making my way here. I know I had my drum, and now that is gone. My pack and a water skin were by my side." I saw a flash of teeth in a beam of moonlight that trickled down through the leaves above us as Abell smiled. "I bet Sergeant Dunkley carried me to safety. Yes, that's it!" Abell seemed cheered by this thought.

My mind felt like a ship that had been knocked loose from its moorings and was being battered and whirled around by a great storm. Abell was one of our enemies, enemies I hated with all my heart. Yet he was just a boy like me. I shuddered when I thought that. I could see so many similarities between us. I sank down again and rested my back against the tree, unsure what to do next.

Abell's grip fell from my arm. Perhaps he was convinced that I no longer would bolt away. "Are you with the militia, or is your home here?" he asked.

I saw no harm in telling him my story, though it took quite some time. He peppered me with questions until finally it came back to where my encounter with him began, my flight to the trees with Angus.

"We have a lot in common then," he said. "I wanted adventure and you did, too, but perhaps you are nobler than I am, as that's all I wanted. You want to protect your family and home. My father was against Mr. Madison's war, but I was so set on going, he knew I'd run away and that the only way he could prevent me was to chain me to a post in the barn." Abell laughed as he said that. "Which he would not do, being a man of gentle disposition."

He groaned again and his voice was tight with pain when he next spoke. "Water . . . could you get me my water skin? I cannot reach it."

The water skin was right on the ground to Abell's left, his hand close by it. That puzzled me, but I got to my feet, walked to his other side, and reached down to pick it up. I caught my foot on a root and would have toppled had I not put down both hands to break my fall. When I righted myself and picked up the water skin, both hands were wet. I wondered whether the water skin had been punctured and had leaked. It wasn't until I raised my free hand closer to my face that I saw it was dark with blood.

Abell saw me looking. "It's just a scratch," he whispered, "just a scratch, nothing more. My mother always says that I bleed more than normal. Just a scratch."

I sat down again, frightened by what I saw, but with no idea what to do, so I handed him the water skin and sat watching.

Abell drank long and deep, then seemed to falter, almost letting the water skin fall from his right hand. I caught it and placed it on the ground between us. He closed his eyes and started to talk — more like whispering — so I had to concentrate to make out his words.

"We're both farm boys, Sandy, and both second sons. I don't know about you, but I've had enough of adventure." He sighed. "There's a girl back home, Abigail Thomas. She gave me a handkerchief when I left, one she'd embroidered with a big letter *A*. She had one, too, and when we marched she waved hers and I touched the one she'd given me where it was stowed safe in my pocket." With the arm that seemed to work, he rooted in his pocket, grunting and hissing at each movement, but finally pulled it free. He held it out to me, seemingly blind to the fact that it was soaked in blood.

I took it and there in one corner was the *A* he had described, beautifully worked in blue stitching. All was silent as I regarded it, thinking what its condition signified.

A crashing erupted in the undergrowth just a little way in front of us. Moving fast, two of John Norton's warriors passed by, not looking anywhere but straight ahead. I nearly called out to them, then the words died in my throat, as I thought what they might do to Abell.

Once they were gone, I let out my breath and said, "We were lucky those warriors did not see us."

"Which warriors?" Abell shook in fear. "I heard noise but saw no one. Have they gone? I have heard how savage they can be."

His words chilled me. Trying to move silently, I waved one hand in front of Abell's face, just inches from his nose. His eyes were open but he did not respond, or ask what silly game I played.

"It's beautiful, isn't it?" he said.

For one brief moment I wondered whether Abell was seeing some vision, but I realised that he meant the handkerchief.

"I would like it to return to its twin."

"You will take it home," I said, trying to put a vehemence in my words to make it so. "In the morning, or when the fighting stops, I'll fetch help and your wound will be treated. Then you will be returned home to see your family and Abigail again." I forced myself to believe this would happen. I wanted it to happen — enemy or not.

Abell tried to smile. "I will," he said, although the words were so quiet that I had to strain to hear them. "In my pack are my fife and a bible that my family gave me when I left. It has our names and our town written on the fly-leaf — Mansfield . . . Mansfield." He kept repeating the name until he coughed, and when he stopped I could see blood on his lips. I did not know what to say and was not even sure that Abell would hear me now. He struggled to speak again, the words spaced far apart, as if they were falling from his throat like pebbles into a brook. "I . . . am . . . so tired . . . so cold."

I reached for him then, put one arm around his shoulders and drew him to me so that his head rested on my shoulder. I grasped his hand with my free one, and felt him weakly squeeze it.

"Tell . . . them . . . I . . . was . . . not alone."

He never spoke again.

I could not stop the tears that came then. I bawled like a baby, not caring if my howling drew the enemy to me. I cried for Abell and his Abigail. I cried for myself. I cried for Angus and Father. I cried for shattered dreams of glory and adventure that had ended with a bloody, broken boy in a wood. I cried for oblivion and was granted it, for I fell into the arms of exhaustion and slept.

* * *

I awoke as the first light of dawn washed over that damned battlefield.

Abell's head had fallen to one side, and in the early morning light I saw how young he was, a beardless boy like me, slight in build. His hair was the same shade of butter blond as Angus had, but his hair was curly, not straight. His eyes were open, staring at nothing. It was as if he floated in a sea of blood, with a huge crater in his side. I marvelled at his courage and felt tears spring to my eyes once more. His sweetheart's handkerchief rested on his thigh. I picked it up and carefully placed it in my pocket. In Abell's pack were the fife and bible he had mentioned. The pages of the bible were well thumbed, and dirty fingerprints marred them. I looked at the fly-leaf. My throat thickened and closed as I read:

Given this day, August 13th, 1813, to our beloved son, Abell, that he might remember us.
Mansfield, Pennsylvania
John and Alice Phillips
Martyn Phillips b. 1790
Anne Phillips b. 1791
Leah Phillips b. 1793
Jack Phillips b. 1794 d. 1798
Abell Phillips b. 1801
Robert Phillips b. 1803

Abell was almost my age, though few would have guessed it on seeing us together. I closed the bible and tucked it inside my shirt alongside the fife. I did not speak aloud, but the words in my head were as good as any spoken oath. I vowed that I would follow Abell's wishes and return his belongings to his family.

No guns fired as I staggered out from beneath the trees. All I heard were the sounds of the Falls and of birds singing. Bodies of the dead and wounded lay where they had fallen — bitter enemies were now brothers in pain and death. Gradually, other sounds flooded my ears. I heard the cries and moans of the wounded. Soldiers and militia — my knees weakened in relief when I saw them to be our own — were picking their way across the battlefield. The mist and morning dew did nothing to hide the devastation. Already a bonfire had been started. The dead from both sides were being flung upon it, for there were too many to bury and the heat of the day was already rising.

"Angus! Father!" I screamed as loudly as I could, but I knew it was futile. Noise was rising and no one would pick out my voice from it. I tried to retrace my headlong flight of the night before, but it was impossible to be exact. I scrutinised the faces of the dead and the wounded as I passed, holding my breath lest I should see Angus or Father there, then letting it out in a deep sigh of relief each time it was not.

The area around the guns in the graveyard was a charnel house. Here the fighting had been fiercest, and here the dead and wounded — British, Canadian and American — lay cheek by jowl, beset by flies that buzzed all around. I fell to my knees and retched at the sight of heads staved in, bloody craters in flesh, limbs blown away. As I rose, the sun glinted on butter-blond hair at the edge of the cemetery. I ran to the body, fearing it would be Angus, for it wore neither a red or blue jacket.

He was lying face down and at first appeared unmarked, but when I heaved him over I groaned at the sight, falling to my knees once more. Angus's handsome, open face looked as if he were asleep, but his left arm was shattered below the elbow, a splinter of bone breaking through the bloodied, lacerated flesh. Flies crawled on the wounds. I batted them away with my hands to no avail. I was so frantic to clear them that I hit Angus's arm. He groaned slightly. He was alive.

I cradled Angus in my arms, and continued my futile battle with the flies, for I did not know what else to do. I was still sitting there when Father found us.

His howl on seeing us sounded as though it was wrenched from his body. I don't know whether he thought us both dead. Angus's stillness combined with my filthy, blood-soaked clothes would have terrified anyone. His joy on finding that the blood on me was not mine, and that Angus lived, was blazing, but being a practical man, he set about ensuring that Angus survived. His words were sparse and clipped, but his face showed his relief.

"Sandy," he said, crouched in front of me, both hands on my shoulders, "they told me that you and Angus had been last seen down here by the guns. I prayed all night that you had found safety when the retreat was called."

His face was grey. Before I could explain that I had only just found Angus, he continued. "Stay with your brother and I will return with a cart — they are taking the wounded to Fort George. Keep him safe."

I followed his gaze to where a group of militia and Norton's warriors were patting down bodies and taking what they could find, not always caring whether their victims were dead or wounded. I nodded that I would do as Father said.

He was not away long. As he returned with a cart, I was happy to see John Lee sitting alongside him.

"Jack?" I whispered, not daring to ask more.

"Came through safe," was Lee's laconic reply. Then he grinned. "On burial duty again, and complaining about it just like before." He leapt down from the cart. "Let's load your brother on and then we'll see who else we can take."

Angus stirred briefly but did not awaken as we moved him to the cart.

"Sandy, go with Mr. Lee and gather up other wounded. Bring them here to the wagon."

I hesitated, my eyes once more on the band of looters. "Father," I said, "I was in the woods for much of the night, with an American." I saw the shock on his face and spoke quickly. "Just a boy, a drummer boy." I was struggling to find words to explain all that had happened.

"Does he live?" Lee asked.

I shook my head and tears ran down my face, cutting through dried blood and dirt.

"They'll find him." Lee nodded towards the burial parties.

"But — " It was hard to explain why I could not let Abell's corpse lie unattended. In the end, I pointed to the looters.

"Scum!" My father spat on the ground. "Where were you?"

Mutely, I pointed to the wood on the left flank.

"We'll go there. It's close to our road to Newark. Come, we can fill this cart as we make our way towards the road."

Abell's body was untouched when we reached it. Father sucked in his breath. "Poor, wee lad," he said. "So far from home." He sighed and gently closed Abell's eyes.

I took the bible and fife from my shirt and the handkerchief from my pocket. "He wanted these returned to his family," I whispered.

Father put his arm around my shoulders and I leaned gratefully in to him. "Can you do that, Sandy? Do you have the heart for it?"

I nodded. "He didn't hear it, but I vowed I would, so I must."

"You're a fine boy," Father said, "but I'd hoped to spare you all this. It changes a man."

I wanted to tell him that I understood now — why he'd tried so hard to keep me from the fighting, but he was all business, calling John Lee to come, asking him to make sure that Abell's body was burned. Lee picked up Abell in his arms and, cradling him like a baby, set off towards the bonfires.

"Come on, Sandy," Father said, patting me on the back. "We've dealt with the dead now. Let's see what we can do for the living."

Every jounce and jostle of that wagon ride to Newark caused the men in the bed of the wagon — some eight or so packed tight together — pain and anguish. Those who remained unconscious like Angus were the lucky ones, although I fretted so much about Angus that I found myself constantly turning round to see that his chest still rose and fell. As for the conscious ones, some tried to muffle their groans of pain, but others could not control themselves. Some screamed, some talked. For one man it was a litany of profanity that he chanted, as if the repetition would keep him safe. Another, a grizzled British veteran, kept calling for his mother, a woman who must be long dead. I did what I could, handing out cups of water and even some hardtack that John Lee had provided. I'll admit to being grateful for that, too, as it was only on seeing it that I realised how hungry I was. Father, grim-faced, drove the horses hard.

There was little time for talk, but gradually we pieced together each other's stories. Father had spent the night helping at the farmhouse where we had taken George Markle, frantic at not knowing whether Angus or I would be amongst the wounded that poured in throughout the battle. He told me of the fierce fighting for the British guns, fighting that lasted until near midnight, when the Yankees held the guns. Even though all appeared to be lost, a final, desperate charge was ordered, only to find that the Americans had fled. Why such a turnabout had taken place was unclear even yet, but Father speculated that their losses were just too great to bear and perhaps the Americans had retreated, intending to return, only to find their advantage lost. It did not matter now. We held the field.

Fort George was chaotic when we arrived, our cart just one of many carrying horrific cargo. A sergeant quickly directed us to where we must go. Father's lips thinned as he whispered more to himself than me, "I am come back to where my sojourn in this colony started. Pray God it ends as well."

If I had thought the battlefield a charnel house, then the barracks where we were sent was worse.

The wounded were stacked in rows, spilling out from a building that was half falling down, waiting their turn to be treated. Father and I unloaded our wounded, adding them to the rows. A burly sergeant darted out from the building, and seeing Father and me standing by Angus, came running over.

He was sweating, all his clothing so blood-spattered that he looked as if he had sustained a mortal wound. "Are there more coming?" he panted.

"Aye, I reckon so," Father said. "We were one of the first away from the field." He hesitated as if unsure of himself. "The one with blond hair — " he pointed to where Angus lay " — that's my oldest son. He's hurt bad."

The sergeant shrugged. "They all are," he said, weariness evident in his voice. "And they're all someone's son." He seemed to notice me for the first time, measuring up my size. "And who is this one?"

"My younger son, Alexander. Sandy," Father said.

"Is he a strong-minded boy?"

I was puzzled by this question.

"Strong-minded and strong-willed, too," Father said with a tired grin as he looked at me.

"I shouldn't do this," the sergeant said, "but if you'll lend him to me for the next little while,

I have need of his strength and size. Then I will make sure your other boy does not wait too long for Surgeon Dunlop to look at him."

Father's wrinkled brow showed his doubt, but I spoke up. "Father, whatever needs to be done, I can do it!"

It was agreed that I was now the British sergeant's boy and that Father would return to Lundy's Lane once he had rested and watered his horses, and would come back when he could with more wounded.

"Come, Master Sandy." The sergeant's tone was jocular, but there was steel there, too. "Let's go in and get started."

Smack in the middle of the room, ankle deep in blood, crouching over a table and wielding a saw on an unconscious man's leg, was a striking man. He was as tall as I was — a rare sight — and had a shock of red hair that stuck up from his head like the comb of an angry rooster. He was young, too, appearing not much older than Morag, perhaps twenty or twenty-one. Without looking up, he roared in a Scottish brogue as thick as Father's when he was angry, "Where's that blackguard Denman? Denman, get your scrawny, pustular arse over here and help me."

"I'm here, Surgeon," the sergeant called, "and

I've found us a fresh and lively body to help out." He dragged me over by the sleeve so that I was in view of his doctor.

"So, you're some use after all!" Dunlop cackled and then addressed me. "Boy, you're our brawn. You lift, carry and hold, no more. Can you do that? And I mean do that without crying for your mama, fainting like a girl, or puling like a babe. Do I make myself clear?" He looked sideways at me, his fingers now busied with a large needle and gut, sewing a flap of skin over the bloody stump he had created.

"I can, sir," I managed to stutter out.

"Well what the hell are you waiting for, then?" he roared, making me jump almost out of my skin. "Carry this one out, and bring me my next victim!"

Sergeant Denman and I scurried to obey. The surgery was quick and brutal work. Dunlop seemed to work like a machine: a cursory examination, a quick decision, and then action. More often than not with all the shattered limbs, it was amputation, and here I discovered why one of my duties was to hold. Each patient was given rum, then a spittle-slick piece of leather was positioned between his teeth for him to bite down on. If an arm was the afflicted limb, then Denman took the shoulders and I the feet and we bore down with all our might to keep the patient from bucking as Dunlop worked. If it were a leg, then our positions were reversed, for Denman knew exactly where to hold and yet keep out of Dunlop's way.

I waited for horror to wash over me, but it did not. I was appalled by what I saw, but it did not sicken me. Rather, it fascinated me that one man held another's life in his hands and acted with such confidence, doing all that he could to ensure that life continued. Surgeon Dunlop might be young, but he was fast, taking little more than ten minutes to remove a limb.

There was no way to keep track of time in that hellhole of a place. We worked continuously, not aware of light changing outside. It stank of sweat, blood, shit, vomit and piss. A black cloak of flies buzzed constantly around, settling on the wounded. Most were too weak to wave them away. Denman was true to his word, and Angus was the fifteenth to be placed upon the table when his turn should not have come up for at least another fifteen. He was awake when we picked him up to move him, his eyelids fluttering as if it were an effort to stay conscious.

I manoeuvred myself so that Denman took his feet.

"Sandy?" Angus whispered, a familiar sweet smile spreading across his face. "You're not hurt?"

"No, Angus," I said. "You told me true and sent me to safety. I just wish that you had got there, too."

His smile broadened, then faltered, "Father?"

"He's safe. He and I brought you and other wounded here. Now he's returned to the battle-field to fetch more."

Angus nodded, then closed his eyes as if drifting off to sleep, opening them only when we placed him on Dunlop's table.

"Surgeon Dunlop?" I asked.

He barely looked up as he scrutinised his tools, readying them for use. "Aye? Why is my brawn talking? Brawn is action and nothing but!" He sounded fierce, but laughter lurked in his voice.

"This is my brother, sir," I said. "Can you . . . can you save his arm?" He took a look and shook his head. "Then may I be at his head instead of Sergeant Denman?" I held my breath, hoping he would agree.

He actually straightened up and looked at me. "You've seen what Denman does by now. But if you slip and let your brother move, it could be the worse for him. Are you sure that you want to do this?"

"I am, sir. He saved my life. Now, I want to help save his."

"Fine words, laddie, fine words." Dunlop gave me a savage grin. "Don't let them be lies."

Angus coughed and spluttered at the rum, but got it down. His teeth bit down on the leather and we were set to commence. I bent double, my hands gripping his upper arms, my head alongside his.

A snort came from Dunlop. "Unorthodox, but perhaps it will work."

I talked the whole time, whispering to Angus what was being done, telling him to hold steady, telling him that all would be well. At the first cut, he bucked a little, but Denman and I kept him down and I felt all of his muscles tense as he, too, fought not to move. His eyes were wild and staring, like the eyes of the pigs when Father slaughtered them in the fall.

Sweat ran so freely Angus's hair was darkened with it. He did not scream like some did, losing their leather gag, but from behind his locked teeth came small whimpers. Those nearly undid me, but I knew that I had to stay strong. Thankfully Dunlop maintained his practised speed and Angus's ordeal was soon over. I winced at the *thud* as Dunlop threw the lower part of Angus's arm to join the other limbs piled in a stinking heap in the corner of the room. As we lifted him gently off the table, he turned his head. "Tell Father I was brave," he said.

His words brought Abell to my mind. "You can tell him yourself," I said, fear making my voice sharper than I intended.

"Laddie," Dunlop's voice rang out. "Brawn! Don't you get any foolish notions about staying with your brother. He takes his chances like the rest and you will be back with my next victim, on the double! Do you understand?"

I nodded.

I did not see Angus for two more days, did not know until Father returned whether he even survived.

Dunlop was a Titan. He did not rest for three whole days, just chopped and sewed and bellowed. He worked Denman and me hard, but made us take breaks when some poor solider would be conscripted to fill in for one of us, while we grabbed food and a few hours' sleep. There were so many patients that they had outgrown Butler's Barracks and were housed in buildings around the fort. The lucky ones had family members who had come to attend them — wives, daughters and sons, some come across the river even from America. Father found me the morning of the second day to say that he would stay with Angus, who had a fever, and that I should come when I could.

Even a Hercules such as Dunlop could not continue as he had been doing, and on the morning of the third day he fell asleep on his feet. Only his arm wrapped around his patient's bunk kept him from falling. Sergeant Denman sent me for clean straw, which we laid at his feet. Then we gently unhooked his arm and lowered him onto it. He did not stir at all.

For the five hours that Dunlop slept, Denman and I did what we could for his patients, fetching water, bringing what little food we could find for those who had the strength to eat, washing, cleaning and picking maggots out of wounds — for those pestilential flies continued to plague us all. We built a bonfire a little way from the barracks and tossed onto it soiled dressings and the severed limbs that Dunlop had thrown in a cavalier manner in the corner, exclaiming, "Another one for the pile!" I shivered, wondering whether I had held Angus's arm one last time.

When Dunlop roused himself, dashed water on his face and changed into the clean clothes Denman supplied, he looked surprised to see me. "Still here, Brawn? I thought you'd be long gone to your brother's side."

"My father is with him, sir." I felt awkward and a bit in awe of the man and shuffled my feet a little. "I did not like to leave in case you had further need of me, so I waited until you could tell me whether you do."

"Brawn, do you have brains lurking in that skull of yours? You seem a most mannerly young man." Dunlop was smiling at me.

I blushed and answered, "I am said to be clever, sir."

"You have done well, Brawn. Better than most men much older would have done. You have a strong will and a strong stomach, too, it would seem — just like me." He winked as he said those last words. He probably meant them as a joke, but I took them seriously and it was then that a kernel of an idea formed.

"So, Brawn, what is your real name?"

"Alexander MacKay, sir."

"Well, Alexander MacKay — " Dunlop stuck out his huge hand " — let me thank you for all you did. You are a fine boy who probably saved many a life. Now go and be with your family."

I needed no more encouragement and raced round the fort until I found Father and Angus. Angus's fever had broken. Father looked tired, having stayed up all night, bathing Angus's burning forehead with water and washing his stump with whisky, a trick he'd learned when he was a soldier, saying it seemed effective in preventing putrefaction.

Many of the wounded were being taken by boat to York, or to stay at Chippawa, which no longer harboured any Americans save the wounded and imprisoned. Neither location was to Father's taste, and once Angus was able to sit up and eat the broth we prepared, he rode to my grandfather's for a wagon to take us back there.

Grandfather was beside himself with joy to see us. We had not been there a day before he started making Angus a hook to replace his left hand.

I was amazed at how sanguine Angus was at his loss. I know that I would have driven all around me mad, blustering and bemoaning my fate.

"I am alive," is all Angus said. He had no smile on his face and it was strange to see him so sombre.

But so many were not. George Markle and Abell Phillips were names I could put to the dead, but there were still many more — those who had died on the battlefield, and those Dunlop could not save and who died of their wounds on the stinking floor of the barracks.

Father, once he saw that Angus was settled, departed for home, riding Madison — whom he declared to be a fine horse but less of a character than Hamish. "I have to tell Mother that both her boys are safe and will return soon."

I helped Grandfather care for Angus, who was soon on his feet again, although a thinner, quieter version of himself. He liked to sit on the bank of the river, staring at the water. When I finished my chores, for I felt it only fair to shoulder the heavier ones and leave Grandfather free to go about selling up his smithy and tools in preparation for his move to Ancaster, I would sometimes join him. We talked little, happy in each other's company but lost in our own thoughts, for we both had much to think about.

My mind dwelt on all that had happened and on Abell. With the war not yet ended, I wondered whether his family even knew what had befallen him, and I was determined that I would get the news to them eventually. Towards the end of August, when it was clear that we would leave soon, I decided that I had to return to the battlefield. I asked Angus if he wished to accompany me, but he shook his head and said, "You go, Sandy. I know what happened there and its cost. I think perhaps you need to see it to make it real." His words puzzled me.

The day was fair, the breeze a little cold despite the sunshine, a hint of the change of season that was coming. I set off after lunch, leaving Angus and Grandfather trying a new harness for the hook that Grandfather had made for him. The walk was easy and pleasant and I found myself reflecting on how different this was from the last time I had made the journey, when a mixture of excitement and fear boiled within me.

Great charred circles from the bonfires of the dead could still be seen on the open space in front of the chestnut woods, but the fences that had been trampled down were now repaired. The gravestones in the cemetery had been righted and new ones had been set there, too. I walked into the woods by Portage Road, thinking to find exactly where Abell and I had passed the night, but one tree looks much like another. I sat down under one and thoughts buzzed in my head like bees: of lives cut short, of others changed forever, and of what Father and Angus had known which I had yet to learn. When I came out, I heard not guns and the cries of men in pain, but children's voices intertwining with the roar of the Falls as a group of them chased a puppy down the slope.

I could not bear to stay there long.

Epilogue

August 1820

It was hard taking leave of them all. I had elected to start my journey early and I was touched to see the whole household there to wave me off. Father stood with his arm around Mother, and she did not weep too much. Angus clasped me to him, and told me that I was to make them all proud and not to worry, as Drew was a fine right-hand man on the farm. Then he laughed and changed that to left-hand man, which made Drew blush and kick at the dirt with his toe.

Mathilda, her arms encumbered with little Angus and with wee John holding onto her skirts, kissed my cheek when I leaned down and embraced her. She whispered that she had so much to thank me for — sending her back to live with our family, and all that had happened since then. I thought but did not say that I had as much to thank *her* for, and not just for helping Father when he was so sick after the battle at Queenston, since it was her love for Angus that had brought back his sunny disposition.

Ellen and Polly, now just as joined as Polly once was with Morag, were quite the young ladies. Both presented me with gifts they had made: a fine handkerchief embroidered with my initials, *AM,* from Ellen, and a journal from Polly, who knows how I love to write. Ellen's gift made my throat thicken as I thought of that other handkerchief, lovingly washed by Mother but still faintly stained from Abell's blood, wrapped safe with the fife and bible in my pack. All were going home now, as I had promised, for I would travel far into Pennsylvania, to Mansfield, before I went to Philadelphia. Letters have been few, but the Phillips family know I am coming and what I carry. Abell's Abigail has married another, but she wants her handkerchief still.

Philadelphia. There I will fulfil my dream, a dream started by Surgeon Dunlop — although I doubt that he will ever know that — to train as a doctor. I have laboured long and hard for this, saving all the money that I could earn by day labouring to pay for my schooling. Father did purchase more land for "his boys," but not for me. Instead, knowing how determined I was to do this and what I am like when I set my mind to something, he gave me the money he would have spent on it.

I am not as headstrong as I was, but I am still stubborn.

I must not forget my teacher, Callum Murdoch. He schooled me in all that he knew, teaching me in the evenings when my work prevented me from attending during the day, and then when we were matched in knowledge, he became my friend — a fellow seeker of knowledge, encouraging me to follow my dream.

Once, just a few years ago, I was flushed with hatred, and dreamed of a glorious war, feeling that I was called to battle. Now I am changed by what I saw, by meeting a boy not very different from me, by seeing the sorrow that war brought to my family and to so many others, American, British and Canadian. Now, I have a different calling — the calling to save lives if I can.

Historical Note

The fighting between British and American forces, which we call the War of 1812, actually took place from 1812 to 1815. For the three years that the war continued, Upper and Lower Canada became the principal battleground for a conflict whose main causes were related to events far from their lands.

The relationship between Great Britain and the new American Republic was a tense one in many ways. The United States of America had gained its freedom from British rule in a bloody revolution only thirty years before. Then in 1803, Britain and France again became embroiled in war. The United States tried to remain neutral, but soon suffered economically when both Britain and France tried to enforce trade embargoes to stop other nations from trading with their enemy. American ships were routinely stopped and searched by both the French and British navies and prevented from reaching their destinations. The British navy, facing a shortage of men, also had the habit of "pressing" American sailors into service on their own ships, taking advantage of the sailors' lack of official paperwork establishing their American nationality.

This action caused huge outrage in the United States, a young country still very conscious of what it had suffered to break free from Great Britain. With anti-British feeling rising, the time was ripe for a group of younger American politicians, the so-called War Hawks, to press for action against Great Britain. They also accused Britain of stirring up trouble among and supporting American Native tribes in their disputes with the American government. American expansionism also played a part, as the rich and tempting British colonies of Upper and Lower Canada lay just to the north, garrisoned only lightly by British troops. It was little wonder that James Madison won the American presidential election in 1812, campaigning on a promise of war with Great Britain. He fulfilled that promise by declaring war on June 19, 1812.

Geographical distance and the comparative strength of the British and American navies meant that the war was never going to be brought directly to Great Britain itself. Instead the war was fought in the British colonies of Upper and Lower Canada, on the Great Lakes and on the sea. American forces invaded both Upper and

Lower Canada several times during the war, trying to gain a foothold there. The British made no attempt to invade the United States, although a daring attack was made on Washington, D.C. in the latter stages of the war — burning down the White House in retaliation for the burning of York (now Toronto) the previous year by American forces.

Great Britain had troops stationed in its Canadian colonies. These soldiers, called regulars, would be the main defence against any American incursions. All able-bodied Canadian men between the ages of sixteen and sixty were expected to be enrolled in the colonial militia, ready to be called to arms should they be needed. Not all, however, would abide by this. For some, it was because their loyalties were divided. The British government, seeking to populate its colonies, had made generous land grants available to attract new settlers. Many of those who received such grants were from the United States and their loyalty lay primarily with their former home. Others did not want to leave their families, and feared the economic repercussions their absence would have on family farms or businesses, or their ability to protect what was theirs should an American invasion occur. Most men had almost no military experience apart from the yearly muster of their militia units. For those who did, it was likely to have been more than thirty years prior in the American War of Independence. Such officers and non-commissioned officers were the backbone of the militia.

Present-day readers are used to learning the events of a war almost as they happen. In the early 1800s it took days — even weeks — for news of battles or troop movements to reach communities or families. Once men marched with the militia, their families would have no means of knowing where they were, or whether they were actively fighting — or worst of all, whether they had been wounded or killed. The most striking example of this lack of communication is that a naval battle took place off New Orleans in early January 1815, two weeks after the Treaty of Ghent had been signed in December 1814 to end the war.

Property, often carved with great effort out of the wilderness, was under constant threat. It could be destroyed or badly damaged if a battle were fought near it, as was the case of the Gage farms in Stoney Creek. Not only were the Americans a threat, but British forces could have a negative impact, too, as supplies were commandeered to feed or supply troops. Many landowners' claims for compensation can be found in both the Archives of Ontario and the Archives of Canada.

With more food and supplies required for the British troops, there were shortages for the civilian population. Some civilians, however, did prosper, earning new income from setting up as merchants to supply the British garrisons.

Fear of the outcome of the war was very real for many. A large number of the settlers in Upper Canada in particular had fled there after the American Revolution. Known as United Empire Loyalists because they had remained loyal to the British Crown, many had fought on the British side during the revolution.

The conduct of the war itself may well seem strange to modern readers. Unlike our "instant" wars, those of this time period were long, drawn-out, fragmented affairs. It took time to get troops into position when their only means of getting into place to face off against the enemy was to march there, if it was impossible to travel by boat. Troops and militia carried their own equipment, such as their musket and shot, but heavy artillery would have to be dragged by horses or, if possible, transported by boat. This meant that military campaigns were often spaced far apart. Campaigns were also hampered by weather, with active fighting seldom taking place in winter. Such gaps meant that the militia often returned to their homes for long periods of time. Even in the summer, men from the militia might be released to attend to their harvests. For the 5th Lincoln, 1813 was a quiet year mainly spent close to home, with some being called upon for small duties such as guarding the inn on Burlington Bay against an American naval attack. In fact, such peripheral duties were the usual employment of the militia even in battles, as the British officers did not think highly of the militia's fighting abilities. Colonel Bradt of the 5th Lincoln did indeed complain that he was nearly killed by the wild shooting and poor aim of his own men.

The War of 1812 is sometimes described as one in which both sides claim victory, but this is not really the case. With the battle of Lundy's Lane in July of 1814, it became clear that an American invasion and occupation of Upper Canada was unlikely to be successful, in part because the Americans had squandered some prior opportunities, but also because the conflict between Britain and France was now over in Europe, leaving Britain with more troops and ships to bolster its efforts against the United States. Fighting continued sporadically for several months, with losses and victories for both sides, but on November 5, 1814, the American forces finally withdrew from the Niagara Peninsula in Upper Canada.

Neither side had gained any territory. The trade grievances and the issue of American sailors being press-ganged into the British navy had for the most part been resolved. The settlers in the Canadian colonies felt more secure with there no longer being an immediate threat of invasion from the United States. Although the war undoubtedly created hardship, both in economic and human terms, one of its effects was that the colonists of Upper and Lower Canada perhaps began to see themselves as more of a nation than a collection of settlers. In the years that followed the war, the role the militia played may have been inflated, but it certainly did contribute to the defense of their colonies.

Timeline of Events Pertaining to this Story

1812

June 18: U.S. Senate passes House bill; U.S. President Madison signs War Bill

June 19: Madison declares war on Great Britain

August 16: Americans surrender Fort Detroit

October 13: General Isaac Brock killed at Battle of Queenston Heights

1813

April 27: Americans capture York

May 27: Americans capture Fort George; British abandon the whole Niagara region including Fort Erie, and retreat to Burlington

June 6: Battle of Stoney Creek

July 31: second occupation of York

December 10: Burning of Newark (now called Niagara-on-the-Lake)

December 18–19: Fort Niagara, across from Fort George, captured by British

1814

July 5: Battle of Chippawa

July 25: Battle of Lundy's Lane

November 5: Americans destroy Fort Erie

December 24: Treaty of Ghent signed

1815

January 8: Battle of New Orleans

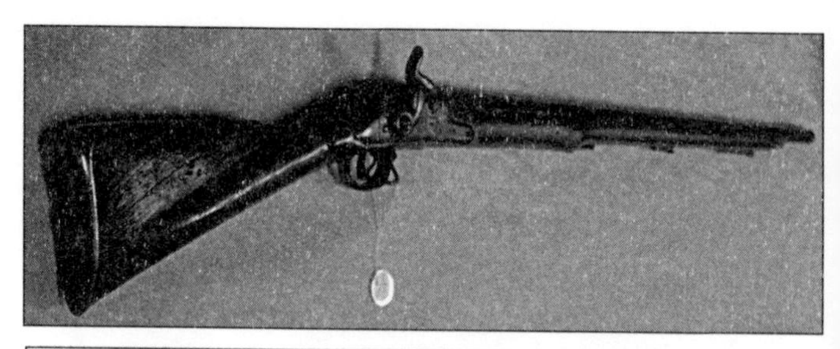

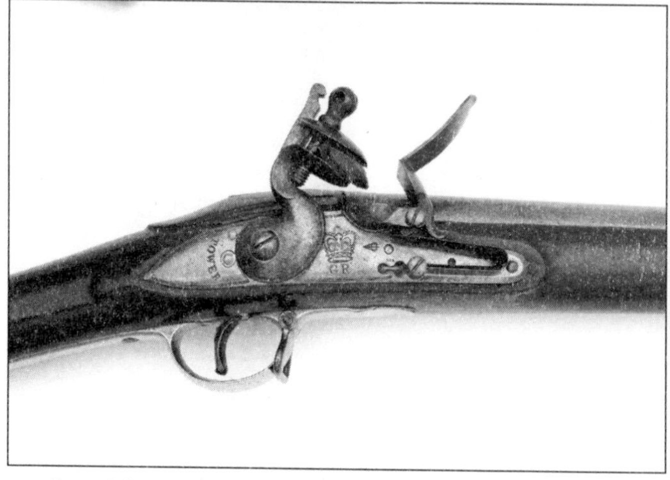

One of the muskets carried by British soldiers in the War of 1812 was nicknamed the Brown Bess. This example is called a Pattern 1793 Ordnance Musket by experts. It could be fired two to three times per minute.

John David Kelly's famous painting, Battle of Queenston Heights, *depicts the death of General Isaac Brock.*

IT HAPPENED IN CANADA
A RARE PRIZE
IN THE LONG HISTORY OF THE BRITISH EMPIRE, THE ROYAL STANDARD (FLAG OF THE SOVEREIGN) HAS ONLY BEEN CAPTURED, BY ENEMY FORCE OF ARMS, ONCE – WHEN THE AMERICANS ATTACKED YORK (TORONTO) IN 1813; DURING THE WAR OF 1812.
12-28
©1978 – Johnson

After the Americans crossed the Niagara River and captured Fort Erie, they overpowered a force of British regulars under General Riall. The British retreated to Queenston Heights. This image shows American soldiers under Colonel Miller.

American General Jacob Brown met the British regulars and local militias at Lundy's Lane on July 25, 1814, in one of the bloodiest battles of the war.

The struggle for the cannons was one of the fiercest of the Battle of Lundy's Lane. Both sides claimed to have won the day, but suffered heavy losses.

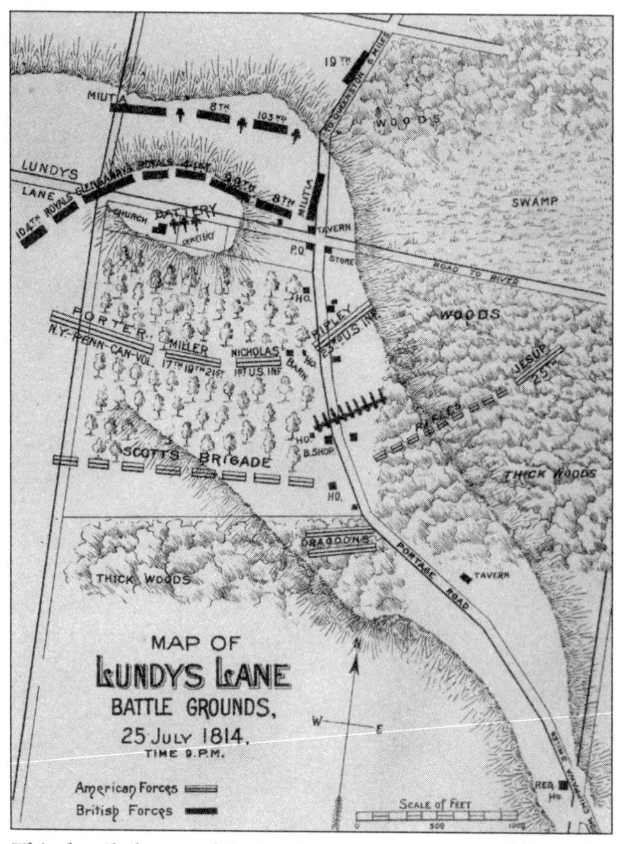

This detailed map of the battlegrounds at Lundy's Lane shows where the American forces squared off against the British regulars and Canadian militia.

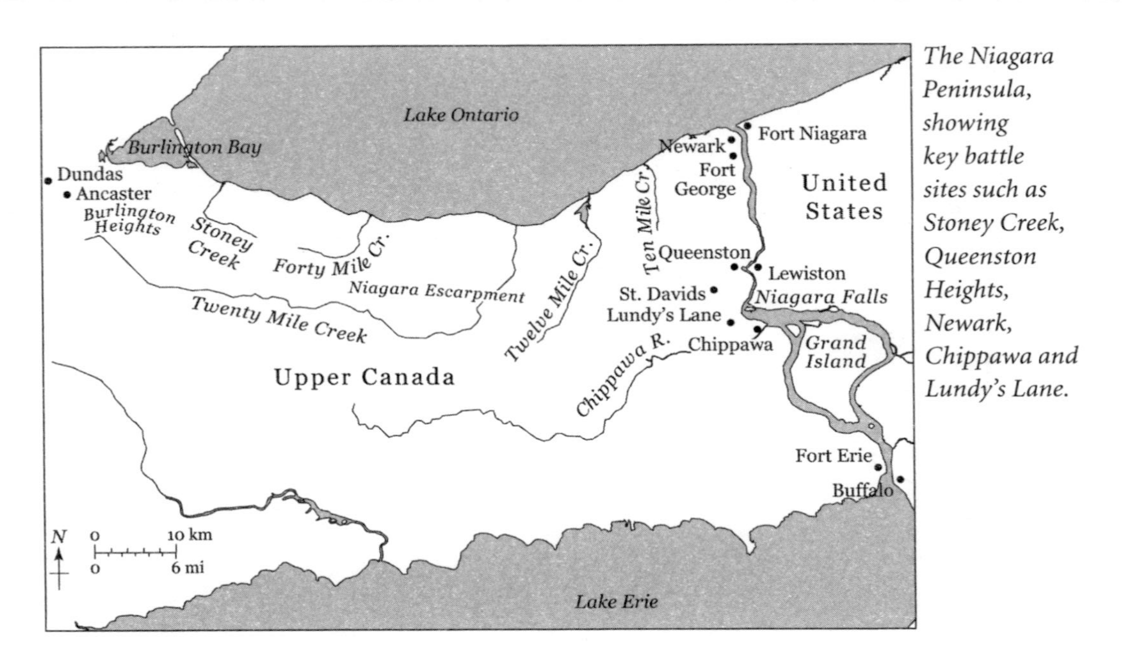

The Niagara Peninsula, showing key battle sites such as Stoney Creek, Queenston Heights, Newark, Chippawa and Lundy's Lane.

Credits

Cover cameo (detail): *Portrait of a Young Man* (oil on canvas) by John Opie (1761–1807) San Diego Museum of Art, USA/ Gift of Bella Mabury in memory of Paul R. Mabury/ The Bridgeman Art Library SD316415
Cover scene (detail) and page 184: John David Kelly, *Battle of Queenston Heights, 13 October 1812,* 1896, National Archives of Canada, C-000273.
Page 183: Brown Bess musket and detail, from *The Brown Bess* by Erik Goldstein and Stuart Mowbray.
Page 185: *A rare prize in this long history of the British Empire...*, Library and Archives Canada, Acc. No. 1993-334-47; copyright: Estate of Gordon Johnston.
Page 186: *Colonel Miller at the Battle of Chippewa;* July 1814, Copy of engraving by W. Ridgway after F.O.C. Darley, circa 1860, ca 1900–1982, National Archives 111-SC-96967.
Page 187: *Battle of Lundy's Lane,* oil on card by Alonzo Chappel, image courtesy of RiverBrink Art Museum.
Page 188: *The Battle of Lundy's Lane,* C.W. Jefferys, [ca. 1921], pen and ink heightened with Chinese white, Archives of Ontario, OSA accession number 621234.
Page 189: *Map of Lundy's Lane Battle Grounds, 25 July 1814, Time 9 p.m.,* Library and Archives Canada/Alfred Sandham, C-096530.
Page 190: Map by Paul Heersink/Paperglpyhs.

The publisher wishes to thank Barbara Hehner for her attention to the factual details, and Dr. Ross Fair, Ryerson University, for sharing his historical expertise.

About the Author

Gillian Chan has lived for over twenty years in the area where many of the decisive battles of the War of 1812 were fought, but her childhood was spent moving around England and Europe as her father, a Royal Air Force officer, was posted to a different base every few years. She's keenly interested in history, and says that if she hadn't become a writer, she'd have been an archaeologist. Being part Celt herself, she is drawn to histories of Scottish and Irish emigrants and is fascinated by their fortitude and sense of adventure.

Stories of the War of 1812 linger throughout the Niagara peninsula — many of them drawing more attention during the bicentennial of the war in 2012. It is impossible to drive through the area without coming across dozens of place names that show up in War of 1812 battle history: Stoney Creek, Lundy's Lane, Queenston Heights, Burlington Bay, Newark, Fort George. Gillian was fortunate to find not only histories of such famous battles, but also the diary of a settler in Ancaster, to give her the flavour of a typical person's life in that era.

She says: "When doing the research, little things moved me — so much so that I had to incorporate them into the book. I was lucky enough to find in the Ontario Archives the diary of Benjamin Smith, who had settled in Ancaster and wrote something every day for many years, even if it was only one line, such as: *Threshed oats in the barn.* His diary gave me an insight into how hard the daily life of a farmer was at that time, and how there was little time — or, indeed, taste — for reacting emotionally, however tragic an event might be. When he and his wife have a child, he records it very matter-of-factly, along the lines of: *Nancy had a son.* No name is given, and then a few days later the brief comment: *Child has fever.* This is followed by: *Child died at 4 o'clock in the morning,* and then: *Buried child at 11:00, Neal* [presumably his brother] *preached.*

"I found myself haunted by these entries."

One of the novel's most graphic scenes is that of the famous surgeon, William "Tiger" Dunlop, sawing off the limbs of wounded soldiers with only spirits for anaesthetic and strong men to hold the patients down. Gillian says she was mesmerized by stories of his prowess. "He is outrageous, larger than life — the sort of man who would be amusing to be with but impossible to live with. Dunlop went to India during the 1820s, but then settled with a lot of his siblings in Upper Canada in the Goderich area. He lived with his brother (also unmarried) and a widow who acted as their housekeeper. When it was suggested that this was not a seemly arrangement, the brothers tossed a coin to see who should marry the woman. The brother lost . . . and married her! The story also goes that Dunlop tricked this brother by using a two-headed coin.

"When Dunlop died in the winter of 1848, the story is that his body was kept in the ice house at Hamilton's Dundurn Castle until he could be buried in the spring when the ground thawed."

Gillian Chan is the author of half a dozen books. Her first, *Golden Girl and Other Stories,* was shortlisted for the Mr. Christie's Book Award. A companion collection, *Glory Days and Other Stories,* was also a Christie nominee, and shortlisted for the Governor General's Award. Her first novel was historical fantasy, *The Carved Box*, followed by *A Foreign Field,* about a World War II pilot. Gillian has written the award-winning Dear Canada title, *An Ocean Apart,* about a girl in Vancouver's Chinatown helping her father try to earn enough money to pay the head tax that will bring her mother and younger brother from China to Canada. *An Ocean Apart* was shortlisted for the Canadian Library Association Book of the Year Award, and won the Arts Hamilton Award for Children's Book. Her most recent novel is *The Turning.* Gillian is currently researching another book for the I Am Canada series, about the siege of Hong Kong during World War II.

What's next for Gillian Chan? Given the topics of her prior books, it's hard to anticipate what will intrigue her. But she has promised her son that at some time in the future, she will write a book about baseball.

Other books in the I AM CANADA series

Prisoner of Dieppe
World War II
Hugh Brewster

Blood and Iron
Building the Railway
Paul Yee

Shot at Dawn
World War I
John Wilson

Deadly Voyage
RMS *Titanic*
Hugh Brewster

Behind Enemy Lines
World War II
Carol Matas

For more information please see the I AM CANADA website: www.scholastic.ca/iamcanada